THE WITCHES OF FAIRHOLLOW HIGH

The SECRET

Also by Ariana Chambers

The Witches of Fairhollow High: The New Girl

THE WITCHES OF FAIRHOLLOW HIGH

The SECRET

ARIANA CHAMBERS

EGMONT

With special thanks to
Siobhan Curham and Catherine Coe

EGMONT

We bring stories to life

First published in Great Britain 2017
by Egmont UK Limited
The Yellow Building, 1 Nicholas Road, London W11 4AN

Copyright © Egmont UK Ltd, 2017

ISBN 978 1 4052 7741 9

www.egmont.co.uk

A CIP catalogue record for this title is available from the British Library

Typeset by Avon DataSet Ltd, Bidford on Avon, Warwickshire
Printed and bound in Great Britain by the CPI Group

59671/1

There was a time when I really looked forward to school trips. When the worst thing I had to worry about was whether one of the boys would be sick on the coach from one too many speed bumps or way too many sweets. But that was before. Before I moved to Fairhollow, my mum's home town, and before my life was turned upside down and inside out with the revelation that I am a witch.

Yes, you read that correctly. And no, I don't fly about on a broomstick or turn people into frogs or eat my dinner from a cauldron. But it turns out that a few families in Fairhollow still carry some kind of witch gene, and mine happens to be one of them. Having the witch gene means you are born with some kind of witch power – like invisibility or being able to harness energy or move through walls. My power is being an empath, which means I can tell how other people are feeling – and sometimes what they're thinking. This is *not* as cool as it might sound. Now everything in my life – including school trips – comes laden with issues. Like how I'm going to deal with the other witch kids at my school who've chosen to embrace the dark side.

'I heard that a girl got murdered in Mad Bess Woods,' Izzy says loudly from the back of the coach.

'Yeah,' Izzy's sulky-faced sidekick, Vivien, chimes in, equally loudly. 'That's how the woods got their name. Apparently she was lured to her death by the ghost of a Victorian orphan girl called Bess. Who was mad.'

Next to me, my friend and fellow good witch, Holly, gives a dramatic sigh. 'If they're going to make up stories, they could at least use a little imagination. Lamest plot ever.'

I can't help laughing. Holly is the biggest

bookworm I've ever known. I bet if doctors looked inside her brain, in the interests of medical science or something, her memory would look just like a library, with shelves and shelves of the books she's read all stored away inside.

'That's right,' Stephen's voice booms down the coach. 'They, like, found her body hanging from one of the trees and she was, like, all dead and stuff.'

Stephen is Izzy's other sidekick. All brawn and no brains. And until recently, no eyebrows, thanks to an 'accident' Holly orchestrated with a Bunsen burner.

I feel a sudden shiver coming from the right of me and I glance across the aisle at Eve. As usual, she's sitting by herself, and staring grimly through her huge glasses at the back of the seat in front of her. She's bolt upright and her face is as white as a sheet. I think about leaning across and asking if she's all right but something stops me. Eve always seems so unapproachable, so self-contained. Instead of saying anything I take a deep breath, relax my body and focus on Eve. I'm going to use my empath abilities to try to pick up how she's feeling. I picture unlocking a huge wooden door in my mind and imagine Eve walking through it. A wave of fear rushes in. It's so intense I have to slam the door shut again. My body fills with concern that's all mine.

'So . . . should be a fun trip,' I say, leaning across the aisle to Eve.

Eve gives the world's smallest nod and continues staring at the seat back.

'What was that, Nessa?' Izzy calls to me down the coach.

I get a sinking feeling. Ever since things came to a head between us in Aunt Clara's kitchen, and Holly and I showed them how strong our powers were, Izzy and the other Blood Witches have been really wary of us. It's been months since she's talked to me.

'Isn't it nice how all the odd ones out end up coming together on a school trip?' Izzy continues.

I turn to look at her. She's all blonde curls and dimples and sweet smile. *Sickly*-sweet smile. If only people knew how evil she could be.

'Yeah, really nice,' Vivien echoes, her thin lips pinched together, sour to Izzy's sweet.

I glance at Holly and she mirrors my frown.

'Just like a flock of sheep,' Izzy says with a giggle.

'Why's she being like this?' I mutter to Holly. 'Why's she being so brave all of a sudden?'

'I don't know. But if she doesn't shut up I'm going to stuff this in her mouth!' Holly pulls a huge hardback book from her bag. '*The Complete Lord of the Rings*,' she adds. '*Eight hundred and seventy-nine pages.*'

I laugh. 'Yep, that should do it!'

'You'd better watch yourself in the woods, girls,' Izzy calls. 'Ghosts love haunting loners like you.'

I glance at Eve. She's still staring straight ahead but her hands are now balled into tight fists in her lap. Then a horrible thought occurs to me and I turn back to Holly.

'Do you think Izzy's being like this because she knows we're going to be miles away from Aunt Clara? Do you think she thinks we'll be weaker without her?'

Holly's face falls. 'I bet that's it. I bet they think they've got the upper hand now there's three of them and two of us.'

I feel sick as I remember everything Aunt Clara told us about the Blood and Silver Witches, and how in each generation they compete to complete their pente – or circle of five witches – first, so they won't lose their powers. At the moment, in our generation, the Bloods already have three witches and us Silvers only have two. Whoever gets five witches first wins and the other witches lose their powers.

'Yeah, well, if they try anything we'll have to show them they're wrong.' I sit up straighter in my seat. In the months since Aunt Clara revealed that she was a Silver Witch too, she's helped Holly and I hone our gifts. Teaching Holly how to harness her ability to control energy (and stop blowing up electrical appliances!) and showing me how to use my empath abilities by visualising a door in my mind to help me block other people's feelings from flooding in.

At the front of the coach, Mr Matthews gets to his feet. As usual, his wiry white hair is springing from his head in every direction and his crumpled suit hangs loosely from his thin frame. He fiddles with the microphone in his hand and a screech of feedback rings around the coach, causing everyone to flinch. 'Whoops-a-daisy,' he sing-songs into the microphone and his voice bellows out through the speakers in the ceiling. I'm not exactly sure why the school decided to send Mr Matthews on this trip. Somehow I can't see him hiking up a storm in the woods. Thankfully our super-sporty PE teacher, Miss Black, is with us too. Maybe Mr Matthews came because he fancied doing some marking in a more tranquil setting . . .

'Exciting news, ladies and gents,' Mr Matthews

says, his mouth a little further from the microphone this time. 'We will shortly be arriving in Mad Bess Woods – let the adventures begin! Oh dear . . .' The coach rounds a sharp bend and Mr Matthews swings straight into the lap of Miss Black. 'I do beg your pardon,' he says, the microphone still on.

I look at Holly and shake my head. 'Something tells me this is going to be the longest three days in history.'

'Yep. Even longer than the weekend I spent with my parents in Berlin when I had nothing but German books to read.'

'I didn't know you could read German.'

Holly sighs. 'I can't.'

The coach starts making its way up a bumpy track into the woods. The sky was already overcast but now, surrounded by towering trees, it's practically as dark as night. The trunks are gnarled and twisted – the kind that look at if they have faces carved into the bark. Tortured, howling faces.

Apparently Mad Bess Woods is one of the oldest forests in the country. It got its name from Lady Elizabeth Thomas who lived in a nearby stately home hundreds of years ago. When her son died at the age of seven she went mad with grief and spent months roaming the woods crying. At least, that's what it said on Wikipedia.

As the coach carries on up the track everyone starts fumbling in the overhead shelf for their coats and bags. Everyone apart from Eve, who's now looking down into her lap, whispering something under her breath. I quickly visualise the door in my mind opening and feel overcome with a sense of gratitude. Eve isn't feeling scared any more – she's feeling relieved. But why?

Finally, the coach pulls into a large clearing. There's a faded sign to our right that says *WELCOME TO MAD BESS CAMPSITE*. Or at least that's what it should say, but most of the B in Bess is missing so it looks as if it says *MADnESS CAMPSITE*.

Holly looks at me and raises her eyebrows. 'I hope that isn't an omen!'

Mr Matthews gets back to his feet. 'OK, everyone, let's disembark with a little decorum. Will the people in the seats at the front leave first, please?'

But Izzy, Vivien and Stephen are already halfway down the aisle. As she reaches our seat Izzy stops and looks down at me. Her pale blonde curls fall in perfect ringlets around her face. Izzy looks really beautiful when you first glance at her but it doesn't take long to see the hardness inside of her poking its way out through her jutting cheekbones and pointed chin.

'Better be careful, freaks,' she whispers. 'Camping can be really dangerous if you don't know what you're doing or what to look out for.'

Hatred starts twisting in the pit of my stomach like a swarming mass of snakes. Crap! Her feelings are breaking through my barrier. I picture the door in my mind but it's wedged open.

Izzy sniggers. 'This is going to be so much fun.'

I hear Vivien laughing behind her and the hatred starts snaking its way up into my throat, choking me from the inside. I look away from them, out of the window, and see a huge tree. It reminds me of my favourite old oak tree back in Fairhollow. I picture sitting beneath it, soaking up its strength and the hatred inside me starts to fade. I slam the door shut in my mind and get to my feet. I can't let the Blood Witches win.

'You don't scare me,' I hiss after Izzy. But she's already stepping off the coach.

Once we've all got off and the coach has chugged back down the path, we gather around the teachers.

Mr Matthews takes a pen from behind his ear. 'OK, so first of all we need to . . .' He frowns and looks at his clipboard. 'We need to . . .'

'We need to put up our tents,' Miss Black cuts in, folding her huge arms in front of her chest. Rumour has it she's a black belt in karate *and* a boxing champ. I'm not sure if it's true but I definitely wouldn't want to get in a fight with her. 'I want you to put them up in a circle around the edge of the clearing and the first ones to finish win a prize.'

Excitement ripples around the group.

'I bet it's something really outdoorsy and boring,' Holly whispers. 'Like a compass.'

'Good, good,' Mr Matthews says, still rifling through the papers on his clipboard. 'OK, on your marks, get –'

Miss Black blows hard on the whistle that's permanently hanging around her neck, causing Mr Matthews to drop his pen in shock.

I look down at the tent at my feet. It belonged to Aunt Clara and my mum when they were kids. When Aunt Clara said we could use it on our trip I was really touched. If your mum dies when you're little you tend to grab on to every memento you can. Holly unzips the bag and slides the tent poles out and we start putting them together. Beside us, Eve starts unpacking her single-man tent and I feel a pang of sorrow. If our tent's big enough I might suggest to Holly that we invite Eve to share with us. I glance across the clearing to Izzy, Vivien and Stephen. You would think that with three of them they'd be almost finished, but they haven't even started. Instead, they're looking around at everyone else with smirks on their faces. Oh, whatever. I pick up the tent tarpaulin and start pulling it over the frame.

'We've finished, sir!' Izzy calls a second later.

I look over in shock. How can they be finished? They haven't even started! But their tents are up and all three of them are standing in front of them beaming smugly.

Mr Matthews looks as bewildered as I feel. 'What? Oh, I say. How on earth . . .?' He starts to chuckle. 'Well done. Well done indeed.'

I look at Holly, my heart sinking as I figure out what's happened. 'Izzy must have time-shifted,' I whisper. As a time-shifter, Izzy has the ability to slow down time.

Holly nods. 'Why'd she have to get that power?' she sighs. 'It's not fair.'

'Can we have our prize, sir?' Vivien asks.

'Yes, yes of course.' Mr Matthews scratches his

head and looks at Miss Black. 'Do you, er, do you know what the prize is?'

Miss Black sighs and reaches into her bag.

I vent my frustration by hammering a tent peg into the ground. Why should they get a prize for cheating? Then I see what the prize is and I start to grin.

'Here you go, girls – and Stephen,' Miss Black says. 'Some bunting to decorate your tent.' She hands them streams of bunting covered in pink bunny rabbits.

Holly starts to giggle. 'What a lame prize! It's even worse than a compass.'

Izzy and the others clearly think so too from the way they're glaring at it.

'Go on, then,' Holly calls over to them. 'Make your tent look nice and pretty.'

Izzy glares at us. I smile back sweetly.

As Holly and I continue putting up our tent I think of my mum and imagine her and Clara going camping when they were our age. I imagine Mum's hands on the canvas where mine are and it makes me feel warm inside.

Next to us, David and James start play-fighting with their tent poles. Spiky-haired David is always fooling around. Seriously, you could send him to a funeral and he'd find a way of making a prank out of it.

Holly looks at me and shakes her head. 'Longest three days in history.'

'Stop it, boys,' Miss Black snaps at them from behind us.

'Sorry, miss,' David says. 'We were just . . .' He breaks off and looks around blankly.

I turn and follow his gaze. There's no sign of Miss Black anywhere near us.

'Did you hear Miss Black?' he says to James.

James nods and stares, confused.

Vivien walks past with a smile on her face. 'Must have been a ghost,' she says.

'She mimicked her,' I whisper to Holly.

Holly nods. 'Another wasted power,' she says

wistfully. 'Still, maybe we don't need to worry about them on this trip if this is how they're going to use their powers.'

Miss Black appears from behind the toilet block on the other side of the clearing. David and James start putting up their tent in silence.

'My rucksack!' Eve calls out, her voice shrill with panic.

I turn to face her. Eve's tent is up and she's looking around wildly. 'It was right here, now it's gone.'

'Are you sure?' I ask, walking over to her. 'You didn't leave it on the coach, did you?'

Eve shakes her head, her eyes wide behind her glasses. 'No, I was just looking in it for the tent instructions. It was right here.' She points to the ground by her feet. 'Someone must have taken it.'

'Is everything all right, girls?' Miss Black calls over.

'No. My bag's gone missing.' Eve looks distraught. 'It's got my phone in and my clothes and everything.'

Miss Black strides over. 'Well, it can't have gone

too far.' She turns to the rest of the group. 'Has anyone seen Eve's bag?'

Everyone shakes their head.

'I don't understand,' Eve says, her voice wobbling. 'It was here just a moment ago. How can it have disappeared?'

I look over at Izzy and she looks straight back at me, her pale green eyes glinting with amusement. 'It must have been the ghost of Mad Bess,' she says quietly.

I suddenly feel a very long way from home.

High up above me in the treetops a crow starts to caw.

'First of all, you need to get your kindling,' Mr Matthews calls.

It's the evening and we're all sat in a circle in the middle of the clearing learning how to make campfires. So far, this has involved hunting around the woods for dry leaves, moss and sticks of all shapes and sizes. Holly and I start putting our twigs and pieces of bark into the small pit we've dug in front of us.

'Make sure it's well spaced out. There needs to be room for the fire to spread.' Mr Matthews starts walking around the circle, inspecting our efforts. He's changed out of his suit into an ancient-looking tracksuit and a battered pair of hiking boots. 'Good job. Good job,' he says as he walks past each of us. 'Now place your tinder on top of the kindling.'

We carefully put our leaves and moss on top of the twigs.

'And now, you may light the tinder!' Mr Matthews announces dramatically, as if he was declaring the opening of Parliament.

'I'll do it,' I say to Holly, grabbing our box of matches. Although Holly's got way better at controlling her energy-harnessing power, there's no way I'm risking getting my eyebrows singed off.

'If you insist,' she sighs.

I strike the match and hold the flame under a

19

clump of leaves. A flame shoots right up. Holly giggles.

'Was that you?' I frown at her.

'I was only trying to help,' Holly says. 'And speaking of which, I wonder how Izzy's getting on.'

We look across the clearing. Tiny flames are licking at their kindling like orange tongues. Holly frowns and scrunches up her nose. The flames splutter out. Stephen lights a match and throws it on the leaves. Once again, some small flames flicker – and once again they die out.

I look at Holly and grin. 'Are you doing that?'

She nods. 'After everything they've got up to today I think it's time they were reminded that they're not the only ones with powers.'

'Good plan!' I say. Although I can't help wondering if using our powers to play pranks is part of being a Silver Witch. We're only supposed to use our powers to do good. Although you could argue that getting one over on Izzy, Vivien and Stephen is a *very* good thing. I watch the flames in Izzy's fire leap up and immediately die out yet again.

'What are you doing?' Izzy snaps at Stephen. 'Here, give them to me.' She grabs the matches from him.

'Oh, this will be good,' Holly mutters, staring at them intently.

Izzy strikes a match and the flame leaps up, almost singeing her fringe. She shrieks and drops the match on to the ground, where it instantly fizzles out.

'Good job,' Mr Matthews says as he crouches down next to us, placing his hand on my shoulder. 'Very good job indeed.' He continues making his way around the circle, inspecting the fires until he gets to Izzy. 'Oh dear.'

'There's something wrong with our matches,' Izzy says sulkily.

Holly laughs. 'What's that saying about a poor arsonist always blaming his matches, sir?'

Mr Matthews smiles. 'A poor workman always blames his tools.'

Izzy scowls.

'Never mind,' I call out to her. 'You guys can't be best at everything. And, hey, at least you won the bunny-rabbit bunting.'

The flames in our fire start leaping about as if they're laughing, blocking the glares coming from the other side of the clearing.

Once we've had dinner – blackened sausages cooked on our fires, which actually tasted surprisingly good – Mr Matthews declares that it's story time.

'Storytelling around a campfire is a tradition that goes back to the dawn of time,' he says. 'It was a way of bonding as a tribe, communicating ideas and –'

'Would anyone like to begin?' Miss Black cuts in.

Izzy nudges Stephen. 'I will,' he says immediately.

Holly groans. 'Seriously? He only knows about twenty words.'

'Once upon a time,' Stephen begins, pushing his floppy blond hair back from his face, 'there was an evil demon who haunted a wood, just like this one.

The demon's name was – was – Bloodbark, and he was the grossest thing you ever saw. He had, like, really rough skin like tree bark and these teeth that were, like, so sharp they could shred human skin in just one bite.'

'Yawn, yawn,' Holly mutters.

Somewhere in the woods behind me I hear a rustle and a twig crack. I hug my blanket around me.

'Bloodbark lived in the trees in the wood. He was actually, like, a wood demon. The evil spirit of the oldest tree in the wood. Just like that one.' Stephen points to a huge old tree at the side of the clearing. As if on cue a chill wind gusts through the clearing, causing the tree's branches to wave and creak. A shiver runs up my spine. Why did Mr Matthews have to suggest this? Why couldn't we have had a sing-song around the fire instead? I wistfully think of my guitar, propped against my bed where I left it after my farewell strum this morning.

'And Bloodbark would creep around the

woods at night-time, looking for campers to kill and possess.' The dying flames from the fire cause shadows to dance on Stephen's face, making it look as hollowed out as a skull.

Somewhere in the distance an owl hoots.

'What was that?' Izzy says. She looks really rattled.

'It was Bloodbark,' Stephen says with a grin. 'That's how you know when he's coming – when you hear him howl.'

'Shut up. It was just an owl,' Vivien says, but she's looking really uneasy now too.

'The thing is,' Stephen continues, oblivious, 'you never know when Bloodbark's going to strike because he looks just like a tree.'

The wind picks up again, causing all of the trees around the clearing to sway.

'And you never know when his branches are going to reach out and grab you.'

We all sit in silence for a moment, listening to the trees swaying and creaking.

'So, what does he do when he catches you?' David asks.

'He, like, sucks all your blood,' Stephen says theatrically.

Holly lets out a loud sigh. 'Boring!'

Stephen glares at her. 'Why's it boring?'

'It's been done already.' Holly shakes her head, causing her curls to bounce wildly. 'Er, hello? Dracula? It would be way better if he captured your spirit and trapped it inside a tree. Then the whole wood could be possessed by the trapped spirits of bitter, dead teenagers.'

I glare at her.

'What?' she mutters. 'That's a way better ending.'

'Could someone else please tell a story?' Eve says, staring into the dying embers of her fire.

'I have one,' Mr Matthews says.

I breathe a sigh of relief and prepare myself for a jolly tale about nature – or marking books.

'It's funny, actually,' Mr Matthews says, sitting up straight. 'It came to me earlier, when I was checking your fires. Which goes to show you just never know when inspiration might strike. Anyway, it's the story of two rival groups of witches.'

I shoot a glance at Holly.

'One group are good witches but the other – they're pure evil.'

I glance across the clearing. Izzy, Stephen and Vivien are looking at each other and frowning.

'Now these witches are in competition. They have to . . .' Mr Matthews breaks off for a moment, as if deep in thought. 'They have to find a bag.'

'What kind of bag?' Eve asks.

'The bag that contains the five most powerful spells.'

I feel a weird unsettled feeling inside. His story is dangerously close to the story of the Silver and Blood Witches. Could Mr Matthews know about it? Could he have heard the folklore?

'And these spells contain the secret to everlasting life,' he continues.

'How many of these witches are there?' I ask casually.

'Oh, thousands,' Mr Matthews replies. 'In the land where my tale takes place, they are all witches – it's just that some are good and some are evil.'

'So it's not set in the present day, then?' Holly asks.

Mr Matthews laughs. 'Of course not. It's about witches! Anyway, where was I?'

As Mr Matthews continues his increasingly fantastical tale of the world of Witchvale, Holly and I exchange relieved glances. It had to just be a coincidence. The wind whips around the treetops and deep in the woods another owl hoots. I pull my blanket tight around me.

The next morning when we all gather to eat breakfast, it looks like a scene from a zombie apocalypse. I'm guessing from the dark circles and bags under everyone's eyes that I wasn't the only one who didn't sleep well last night. Thanks to our 'bedtime stories' I ended up having a nightmare about a tree demon that was trying to steal my guitar from me. 'You'll never, like, play it again,' it yelled – in Stephen's voice. 'You're doomed to live a life without music.' I'd woken in a cold sweat and lay in my sleeping bag rigid as a corpse as I listened to the rustling and creaking from the woods. I don't think I've ever felt so relieved as when the first pale light of dawn started creeping inside the tent.

'Well, on the positive side, we only have one more night to get through,' Holly says, grimacing as she takes a mouthful of cold baked beans. 'Eew!'

'Yep. And one more day.' I glance across at Izzy, Vivien and Stephen. They're huddled together deep in conversation. I wonder if they're plotting what tricks to play this time. I take a deep breath and think of Aunt Clara and how she'd hugged me when I left and whispered the Silver Witches' incantation: Silver me, Silver you, Silver us, Silver true. I feel a shiver going up my spine. Yesterday Izzy and the others caught me off guard, but not today. Today I'll be ready for them. I watch as Eve trudges over to Miss Black. She's wearing the clothes she came in as her rucksack still hasn't turned up. She says something to Miss Black and Miss Black blows her whistle to get us all to be quiet.

'Do any of you girls have some spare clothes you could lend Eve, please?'

Izzy and Vivien immediately start giggling.

Miss Black glares at them. 'Is something wrong, girls?'

Izzy shakes her head, her perfect ringlets bouncing. 'No, miss.'

'Well, what's so funny?'

'Nothing. It's just that . . .' She pauses and smiles sweetly. 'I don't think Eve would really suit any of my clothes.'

'I don't think they'd fit either,' Vivien adds, looking at her thin legs stretched out on the ground in front of her.

Eve's face flushes. Her usually neatly bobbed hair is all flat on one side from sleeping and she looks tired and drawn.

'You can borrow something of mine,' I call across.

'Thank you, Nessa,' Miss Black says.

'Creep,' Vivien mutters.

Izzy and Stephen just smirk.

Eve trudges back across the clearing. 'Thanks,' she murmurs, looking down at the ground.

I crawl over to our tent and pull a clean T-shirt

and some clean underwear from my bag. Thankfully Aunt Clara insisted on me bringing spares of everything. 'You never know when you might need it,' she said. I bundle the clothes up and hand them to Eve.

'Thanks,' she mutters again and disappears off into her tent.

Miss Black blows her whistle again, causing Mr Matthews, who's sitting next to her, to spill his cup of tea all over himself.

'Right,' Miss Black barks. 'The shower block is open for those of you who want showers.' The boys all laugh and shake their heads. 'You have half an hour to get clean and then it's time for our hike to the caves.'

Izzy and Vivien groan in stereo.

'How far is it?' Izzy asks, pouting.

'It's three K,' Miss Black replies. 'Barely any distance at all.'

Izzy arches her thin eyebrows. 'Three kilometres is miles!'

'It's one point eight miles,' Miss Black retorts, getting to her feet and brushing the twigs and leaves from her tracksuit. 'As I said, barely any distance at all.' She puts her hands on her hips. 'Now, when we get to the caves we're going to split into two groups. Half of you will be with me and half of you will be with Mr Matthews.'

Mr Matthews nods his head eagerly. Much as I like him, I'm kind of hoping I'm in Miss Black's group. Mr Matthews is so scatty I can't imagine it would take much for him to get lost.

'It's very important that you all stay together in your allocated groups while we explore the caves,' Miss Black continues. 'The floors are likely to be very slippery and uneven. So no running and no fooling around. Do you understand?' She glares at us and we all nod meekly – apart from Stephen who sighs, like he's the world's greatest action hero, and Izzy and Vivien who exchange sly smirks. My heart sinks. Surely they wouldn't be stupid enough to pull one of their stunts inside the caves? But then I think back to what they did in Aunt Clara's kitchen and how they nearly set fire to the entire building. Of course they'd be stupid enough. I look at Holly to see if she's thinking the same and her grim expression confirms it.

Miss Black starts reading out the names for each group. Holly, Eve and I are in Mr Matthews's group, along with Izzy, Stephen and Vivien. Great. But at least if they do try anything stupid we'll be there to stop them.

After a freezing-cold shower in the shower block, which somehow managed to leave me feeling grubbier than before, we set off for the caves. Miss Black's group have marched on ahead of us and are now out of sight but Mr Matthews prefers a more leisurely approach. It's less of a hike and more of a meander really, as he stops to tell us what every single flower, plant, bird and tree are en route.

'Look! Look!' he cries as we round a bend in the track. 'A toadstool ring!'

There, in a small clearing, is a perfect ring of

toadstools. They're the red and white spotted ones that I've only ever seen in drawings before.

Izzy leans against a tree and sighs like we've just scaled a mountain rather than ambled as slowly as snails.

'Ancient folklore believed this to be a fairy ring,' Mr Matthews continues. 'That fairies would come and dance inside.'

Stephen groans. But I can't help finding Mr Matthews's enthusiasm infectious. All of his little anecdotes are really bringing the woods to life and, unlike the stories last night, in a good way.

'Can we just get to the caves, please?' Vivien says sullenly.

'What?' For a moment, Mr Matthews looks as if he's forgotten the whole purpose of our walk. 'Oh yes – yes of course.' He holds his clipboard aloft. 'This-a-way. Follow me!'

'If we actually find these caves with him in charge I'll eat my copy of *Watership Down*,' Holly mutters.

What feels like two hundred bird, tree and flower sightings later, we make it to the caves. Miss Black's group are sitting on the ground looking bored.

'Where have you been?' Miss Black snaps.

Mr Matthews looks genuinely puzzled. 'Following you.'

'We got here half an hour ago. What took you so long? Oh, never mind, you're here now.' Miss Black blows on her whistle, even though there's no need as we're all sat in silence. 'OK, guys, remember what I said. You must stick together at all times and no running or messing about. I'll go at the front and, Mr Matthews, can you bring up the rear, please?'

'Of course.'

'Now, it will get pretty narrow in there in places. None of you are claustrophobic, are you?' Miss Black looks around the group.

Stephen frowns. 'What does that mean?'

'A fear of small places – you know, like your brain,' Holly mutters.

'Shut it!' Stephen snaps and he, Izzy and Vivien glower at us.

Miss Black starts leading us all into the entrance of the cave. Annoyingly Izzy, Vivien and Stephen hang back so they're right behind Holly, Eve and me at the end of the group. At first the cave doesn't seem too bad. A shaft of sunlight has burst through the clouds and it shines pale yellow on the walls. But as Miss Black leads us further in, the caves start to get narrower and darker. Behind us, Mr Matthews turns on his torch. The beam casts around, eerily reflecting on the stalactites that are shimmering with damp. Up ahead of us, David lets out a ghostly howl and the hairs on the back of my neck stand on end.

'Stop messing about!' Miss Black barks from the front of the group.

'Stop messing about!' she barks again from right behind me, causing me to almost jump out of my skin.

'My goodness, there's a powerful echo in here,'

Mr Matthews says. But I hear Vivien giggling and know that she's been mimicking again. In the darkness, I feel Holly grab my arm and squeeze it tightly. *It's OK*, I tell myself. *They aren't the only ones with powers. We're just as strong as they are.* But in the cold, damp darkness it's getting harder to believe. What if Izzy pulled her time-shifting stunt right now? What if she did something that got us all lost in here? How would I be able to fight back? My eyes frantically search the gloom in front of me and I see a pinprick of light way up ahead. As I edge up the slippery tunnel, the pinprick grows to the size of a thumb. We must be getting near to the exit.

'Nearly there!' Miss Black calls from the front.

I hear Eve sigh with relief beside me and the tension in my body starts to ease. But then I hear a weird rumbling sound.

'Oh great, a thunderstorm,' Holly says.

There's another rumble and something hard hits my face. 'What was that? What's going on?' I turn back to Mr Matthews.

'Bits of the roof are crumbling,' Holly says.

Mr Matthews points his torch upwards. There's another huge rumble. I look at Izzy. Is she doing this? But Izzy looks as shocked as I feel. Vivien and Stephen are staring at the roof of the cave too, looking equally scared. As I turn back, a massive chunk of the roof breaks off, hitting the floor behind us with an almighty crash.

The light up ahead is snuffed out.

4

I crouch down on my heels, trying to stay calm. But fear is closing in on me like the cave walls. It feels as if all of the oxygen is being sucked out, sucked from my body, like a deflating balloon. I try to take a deep breath and it feels as if my airway has been blocked.

'Are you OK?' Holly whispers, crouching down next to me.

I nod, gasping for air.

'Oh dear,' Mr Matthews says, his voice faint and woolly.

'I can't – I can't breathe,' I splutter.

Holly puts her thin arm round my shoulders. 'Are you picking up on everyone else's panic?' she whispers. 'Try to block it out.'

I try to picture the old oak tree but all I see is darkness. I close my eyes. I picture myself walking along the sunlit path to the tree. I picture light and space all around me. And then, finally, I can see the tree. I see its huge roots, like arms reaching out to me. And I picture myself running to sit inside them, pressing my back up against the trunk. Feeling the bark against my skin. Feeling the strength of the tree rushing into me, forcing out all of the fear. I take a deep breath and my lungs fill with air. I open my eyes and now, instead of total darkness, I see the light of Mr Matthews's torch flickering around the cave.

I look at Holly and give her a weak smile. 'Thank you.'

One thing I know for sure is that Izzy and the others can't have been behind the rockslide. I was picking up way too much panic and fear from them. I turn and, sure enough, Izzy and Vivien are huddled together against the wall of the cave. Even in the darkness I can see that they're trembling.

'Where's Stephen?' Mr Matthews asks. 'He was right in front of me. Now he's gone!' He shines his torch around and the light picks up Izzy, Vivien, Eve, me and Holly. Stephen has vanished.

'He must have ghosted,' I whisper to Holly.

She nods. 'Typical of the Blood Witches to only look out for themselves,' she mutters. 'If I'd been given the power to travel through things I'd never have left you.'

'Me neither.' I look back at Izzy and Vivien and wonder what they must be thinking of Stephen for leaving them. They definitely don't look happy.

'He must have slipped through when I wasn't looking,' Mr Matthews says, fumbling around in his jacket pocket and pulling out his ancient mobile phone. 'OK, the important thing is not to panic. I'll call for help and they'll have us out of here in a jiffy.'

'There's no way you're going to get reception in here,' Izzy snaps. 'What if more of the roof collapses? What if we're crushed?'

Vivien whispers something in her ear and Izzy suddenly goes all still and super-concentrated. I wonder if she's trying to use her power. When Aunt Clara explained all of the different witch powers to us she said that, eventually, time-shifters are able to turn back time. I wonder if that's what Izzy is trying to do now. So far she's only been able to slow time down. Izzy continues to focus on the rock in front of her but nothing happens. I turn back to check on Eve. After the way she was on the coach yesterday, I wonder if she's scared of small spaces. This must really be freaking her out.

I edge closer to her.

'Are you OK?' I ask. But Eve doesn't respond. I feel a stab of irritation. I get that she's stressed but we all are. She doesn't have to be so rude. I look back at Izzy. She's staring at the rock in front of us.

Suddenly the rock judders and then it slides to the side, slowly at first and then with a huge jolt it lurches free, leaving a gap just big enough for us to crawl through.

'What on earth?' Holly mutters.

'It's another rockslide!' Vivien shrieks.

'Get out of the way!' Izzy shoves me to one side and crawls through the gap. Vivien is hot on her heels. Eve follows them.

A new horror grips me. Did Izzy do this – when she was staring at the rock? Did she make it move? But how? Could she be more powerful than we thought?

'It's a miracle!' Mr Matthews cries. 'Come on, girls, let's get out of here while we can!'

I look at Holly. 'Did you see that?'

She nods. 'Come on.'

As I crawl through the gap after her I'm struck by a horrible realisation. If Izzy is able to move rocks as well as time-shift we really have got a problem.

That evening, back at the campsite, everyone is still buzzing from what happened in the caves. The teachers have no idea it was anything to do with Izzy. Miss Black thinks it was down to another tremor and Mr Matthews is referring to it as 'The Mad Bess Miracle'. I watch Eve as she goes over to the teachers' barbecue.

'Hey, Eve, you can have some of our food if you like,' Izzy calls out across the clearing.

The chattering dies down. Everyone looks as shocked as Eve to see Izzy being friendly to her. I hold my breath and wait for the inevitable snide remark or prank.

'Seriously.' Izzy takes a burger from their barbecue and puts it in a bun. Then she stands up and takes it over to Eve.

'There's got to be something wrong with it,' Holly mutters and I nod.

'Thanks,' Eve says, taking the burger and turning to head back to her place.

'Hey,' Izzy grabs her arm. 'Why don't you eat with us too?'

'Yes, come and join us,' Vivien calls, making a space on their blanket.

'After what we went through today, I feel like

we've totally bonded,' Izzy says with a smile.

'Is she for real?' Holly whispers.

'Yeah, funny how they don't seem to have "totally bonded" with us,' I reply.

Stephen heads back from the toilet block. He's carrying something.

'Look what I found,' he calls, holding it up. 'Eve's rucksack.'

Eve gasps with joy.

'That's marvellous!' Mr Matthews cries. 'Oh what a happy, happy day this has been. Apart from when we were trapped and thought we might die, of course.'

'Where was it?' Miss Black asks.

'By the toilet block,' Stephen replies, handing the backpack to Eve.

'But – but – how did it get there?' Eve stammers.

'Who cares how it got there?' Izzy says sweetly. 'The main thing is, you got it back!'

Eve hugs the backpack to her and smiles gratefully at Stephen. 'Thank you!'

'Aw, I'm so happy for you!' Izzy exclaims, putting her arm round Eve's shoulders.

'Oh my God. If she doesn't stop with the PDAs I'm going to hurl up my hotdog!' Holly says, shaking her head with disgust.

I look around at the others. They're all as baffled as I am by Izzy's sudden display of affection towards Eve.

'But how did the rucksack get there?' I ask pointedly.

'It doesn't matter,' Vivien hisses. 'All that matters is that poor Eve has it back.' She pats the blanket next to her again. 'Come on, Eve. Come and join us.'

Eve follows Izzy and Stephen over and sits down on the blanket. She looks about as comfortable as a mouse that's just entered a lion's den.

For the rest of the evening we have to watch as Izzy, Vivien and Stephen launch a suck-up fest in Eve's honour. It's not until we get in our tents to go to sleep that I finally get the chance to speak in private to Holly.

'Why do you think they're sucking up to Eve?' I say as soon as we've zipped up our tent and climbed into our sleeping bags.

Holly shrugs. 'I don't know. All I do know is that it must be bad.'

I burrow down deeper into my sleeping bag but it's impossible to get warm. The uneasy truce that seemed to exist since the fire is definitely over. The Blood Witches are up to something, and their powers are greater than we thought. I hug myself tightly and prepare for another night of fitful sleep.

5

As soon as the coach gets back to school, Holly and I hotfoot it down to Aunt Clara's bookshop and café, Paper Soul. As we race along the High Street past The Cup and Saucer I hear a shout.

'Hey, Nessa!'

I turn and see Niall clearing one of the tables outside. My face flushes. But I don't have time to think about the way the muscles in his arms flex as he picks up the tray of cups or how cute his dark curls are as they tumble around his face. I have to talk to Aunt Clara about what happened.

'Hey,' I call back, hurrying past.

'Didn't you know that it's rude to stare?' Holly shouts at him.

'What did you say that for?' I mutter, my cheeks flushing even redder.

'He was gawping at you like a goldfish. Next thing he'll be wolf-whistling. It's not the 1970s you know. We are in the third wave of feminism. Or is it the fourth?'

'Yes, but . . .' I break off. There really is no time for this now. We reach the end of the High Street and I see Paper Soul looming in the distance, its black and red sign swaying in the breeze. It's weird to think that just a few months ago I was arriving here for the first time and it all felt so weird and unfamiliar. Now it practically feels like home. I feel a pang of sadness as I think of my dad working out in Saudi Arabia. It feels like home, apart from my dad.

As we get to Paper Soul Aunt Clara is in the doorway, turning the open sign to closed. She's wearing a long turquoise tunic over black leggings, which makes her flame-red hair look even brighter. Her face breaks into a huge smile as soon as she sees us. I can't stop grinning either and again it feels so weird to think of how awkward it was between us when I first got here.

'Girls!' Aunt Clara cries, coming out and flinging her arms around both of us. 'How did it go? Was it . . .? Were they OK?'

'Not exactly,' I reply, hugging her tightly and breathing in the scent of her rose oil perfume.

'But it was nothing we couldn't handle,' Holly quickly adds as we follow Aunt Clara into the shop.

Even on a sunny day like today Paper Soul stays steeped in darkness, its walls and alcoves lined with books. We follow Aunt Clara through the bookshop to the café at the back. As usual, it smells of incense and bread. For the first time all weekend I start to feel relaxed.

'So, what happened?' Aunt Clara asks, pulling out chairs for us at the nearest table.

'What didn't happen?' Holly says theatrically.

I immediately sense a wave of concern

from Aunt Clara. She looks at me and raises her eyebrows. 'Nessa?'

'Well, there was this rockslide . . .'

Aunt Clara sits bolt upright. 'What rockslide?'

'Oh, it's OK,' Holly says. 'We got out. Well, obviously we got out, or we wouldn't be sitting here, would we? But it was *how* we got out that's the worrying part.' Holly turns to me. 'You tell her.'

'Yes,' Aunt Clara says, also turning to me. 'Tell me everything.'

'We'd gone caving and there was a rockslide and some of us got trapped,' I say quickly, trying not to make too big a deal of it.

Aunt Clara shakes her head in disbelief. 'And were the Blood Witches behind this rockslide?'

'No. Definitely not. They got trapped with us.'

'Apart from Stephen, the big chicken,' Holly says. 'He used his ghosting powers to get out.'

'So, what happened?' Aunt Clara asks. 'How did you get out?'

'Well, we were trapped but then Izzy stared at the

51

rock that was blocking our way and it – it moved. It moved to the side. I don't get how that possibly could have happened naturally. Boulders don't move to the side by themselves. They fall down by themselves but not to the side. That's defying all the laws of gravity. Izzy must have moved it with her powers.'

Aunt Clara whistles. 'But I thought Izzy was a time-shifter not telekinetic.'

'Teleki-*what*-ic?' Holly asks.

'It's when you're able to move objects with your mind,' Aunt Clara explains.

'Do you think it's possible for a witch to have more than one power?' I ask, dreading that the answer might be yes.

Aunt Clara frowns. 'I don't know. I've certainly never heard of it happening before. But maybe the Blood Witches' powers are increasing.' She sighs. 'Oh dear, this is very worrying. Was anyone hurt – in the rockslide?'

Holly shakes her head. 'I think poor Eve must

have gone home traumatised though.'

Aunt Clara looks at me questioningly. 'Eve?'

'Eve Hart,' I say. 'She was trapped in the cave with us too. And she lost her bag.'

'Yeah, and then the Blood Witches randomly befriended her,' Holly adds. 'So, all in all she had the camping trip from hell.'

'Eve Hart?' Aunt Clara says slowly, like she recognises the name.

I nod.

'Do you know her?' Holly asks.

'Didn't you hang around with Eve before Christmas?' Aunt Clara asks me and I start to blush.

Holly frowns. 'Did you?'

I shake my head. 'No. It was when I was secretly seeing you. When . . .' I can barely bring myself to look at Aunt Clara. 'When you told me I couldn't, you know, see Holly. I – er – I pretended I was with Eve.'

'Oh.' Aunt Clara frowns.

'*Awk-ward!*' Holly says in a sing-song voice and

we all start to laugh. 'Seriously though, I'm glad you like me now,' Holly continues. 'It makes life so much easier.'

'It wasn't that I didn't like you,' Aunt Clara says quickly. 'It was just that I didn't want Nessa getting caught up in the Fairhollow witch feud. I was in denial, I guess you might say.'

We all laugh again and I feel a circle of warmth glowing around the table. It's so nice to be home and to be back with Aunt Clara and away from Izzy and the others.

'What did you say Eve's surname was?' Aunt Clara asks, playing with the cat's-head ring on her little finger.

'Hart. Why?' I study her face.

'She hasn't lived in Fairhollow very long,' Holly adds. 'She only started in school last September.'

Aunt Clara nods. 'There was a Silver Witch with the surname Hart who lived here a long time ago. I remember my grandmother talking about her.' Her eyes widen as if she just worked something out. 'She was a telekinetic too. One of the most powerful telekinetics there has ever been apparently. My grandma was in awe of her.' Aunt Clara's expression grows serious. 'But she lost it all when the Blood Witches formed their pente first. That was such a terrible time.'

I feel a shiver running up my spine. Aunt Clara never talks about what happened back when the Blood Witches were in control and I don't want to ask. I can imagine only too well how horrible it must have been. Then something else occurs to me.

'But if your grandma's friend was telekinetic . . .'

'And Eve's related to her . . .' Holly says, as if reading my mind.

'Then Eve could be . . .'

We both look at Aunt Clara.

'You say that Eve was trapped with you in the cave?' Aunt Clara says.

I nod.

'Is there any way it could have been her who moved the rock?'

I close my eyes and try to remember what happened. I see Eve crouching down. But then I looked at Izzy. The next time I noticed Eve was when she was crawling out. 'I don't know.'

'Oh my God!' Holly exclaims. 'Maybe that's why the Blood Witches are being so nice to her.'

'What do you mean?'

'Well, maybe they realised that Eve moved the rock. They realised that she's a witch and –'

'They're trying to get her to join them.' My heart sinks as the pieces of the puzzle fall into place. If Eve does join them they'll only be one witch away from completing their pente.

'We need to find Eve,' I say. 'If she is related to your grandma's friend and she is a witch we need to get her to join us.'

'Before Izzy and the others get their claws into her,' Holly says, getting to her feet. 'Maybe we could find her address online.'

'No need for that,' Aunt Clara says. 'I'm sure I had a Hart come in here to order a book not long ago. She would have given me her address.' Aunt Clara goes over to the counter and starts looking through a leather-bound book. 'Yes, here we are. Hart. Number three, Hollow Hill.'

'Let's go,' Holly says.

'I'll see you later,' I say to Aunt Clara before rushing after Holly through the shop.

'Don't do anything too hasty,' Aunt Clara calls after us. 'You don't want to . . .' But her voice is drowned out by the jangling bell above the door.

6

'Wow!' Holly says as we gaze up at number three, Hollow Hill. The house is set apart from the others, at the bottom of the hill, surrounded by a rambling garden full of flowers. It has a thatched roof and large sash windows, apart from the windows under the eaves, which are smaller and glinting in the light of the setting sun. They remind me of a pair of eyes.

'That's exactly how I imagine my future-life-as-a-writer's house,' Holly says wistfully.

I look at her questioningly. 'Your what?'

'The house I'm going to have when I'm a famous author.' Holly frowns. 'Why are you staring at me like that?'

'Nothing. It's just . . . with all this stuff about being witches, I didn't realise we could still dream of doing other things too.' I think of my guitar. It's been ages since I thought of one day becoming a professional musician.

'Of course we can!' Holly exclaims. 'We just have to make sure the Bloods don't complete their pente. Then we'll be free to do whatever we like. Come on.'

I follow Holly up the winding path. Clusters of daffodils bob in the breeze. It all looks so normal and nice – so un-witchy. Two huge terracotta pots full of pansies stand either side of the front door. I think of how Eve always is in school. Hunched over, trying to make herself even smaller, peering out fearfully from behind her glasses. I would never have imagined her living in a house like this – a house so bright and colourful and cheery. Holly presses the doorbell. Inside the house it plays a jaunty little tune.

'I'll get it,' a woman's voice calls and the door

swings open. 'Hello.' The woman looks at us curiously. She's wearing an apron over her jeans and T-shirt and her hair is tied back in a ponytail. 'Can I help you?'

'Yes – er – we're here to see Eve.' I hold my breath. What if Aunt Clara was wrong? What if this is a different family of Harts?

'Eve?' The woman looks shocked.

'Oh, sorry, I think we might have the wrong address,' I say hastily.

'No –, no –, you haven't, it's just . . .' She breaks off. 'I . . . We weren't expecting any visitors. She's only just got back from a school trip.'

'I know,' Holly says. 'We were on the trip with her. We're in her class. She lent me a book while we were away and I forgot to give it back. So we thought we'd come round to, you know, give it back.'

'Oh, I see,' the woman says, smiling. 'OK, well, I can take it for her.' She holds her hand out to Holly.

Holly's face falls.

'We also wanted to make sure she was OK – after the accident,' I say.

'Oh.' Eve's mum looks at us for a moment. 'Did she tell you, then?'

I nod, wondering what she means. Maybe she thinks we weren't involved in the rockslide, that we weren't there when Eve got trapped. I decide to use my empath abilities to try to read what she's feeling. I picture opening the door in my mind. Sadness shimmers from Eve's mum like pale moonlight.

'Come in,' she says, opening the door wider and stepping back into the hall.

Holly and I follow her inside. I frantically try thinking of something to say if she calls Eve to come and see us but instead an alarm starts bleeping from a room off to the left of the hall. Eve's mum instantly looks stressed. 'Go on up, girls. I need to see to George. Just keep following the stairs to the top of the house.' She hurries off into the room.

I look at Holly. 'Who's George?' I whisper.

She shrugs. 'How should I know? You're the

mind reader! Come on.' Holly starts taking the stairs two at a time. There's one of those stairlifts at the bottom of each landing. The kind that old people have. I wonder if Eve lives with one of her grandparents. 'Maybe George is her granddad,' I whisper to Holly and she nods. By the time we've got to the third floor, I've painted a complete family portrait for Eve, complete with disabled grandfather.

The landing on the top floor is a lot narrower than the one below and there are only two doors coming off it. Both of them are closed.

'What now?' I whisper to Holly.

'Hello!' she yells at the top of her voice making me jump. 'Eve!'

'Did you have to yell so loud?' I hiss. 'You nearly gave me a heart attack!'

There's the sound of fumbling from behind one of the doors and it flies open. Eve stands in the doorway staring at us. She's wearing a stripy tiger onesie and she's taken off her glasses. She looks totally different – and really confused.

'What are you doing here? How did you get in?'

'We need to talk to you about something,' I say. 'Your mum told us to come up.'

Eve frowns. 'She did?'

'Yep. Is it OK if we come in?' Holly gestures to Eve's bedroom.

'Oh. Well . . .' But before Eve can say any more, Holly has walked past her into the room. 'Cool house,' she says.

Eve looks at me helplessly, then gestures at me to go into her room too.

'So, what did you need to talk to me about?' she asks, walking over to the window. I realise that it's one of the tiny ones up in the eaves.

Holly looks at me and nods.

'Is it OK if we sit down?' I say, looking at the cushion-covered bed. Now we're here I don't have a clue what to say. There's always the chance that Eve isn't related to Aunt Clara's grandma's friend. And even if she is, there's always the chance that she didn't inherit her witch powers. How can I find out without appearing totally insane?

'OK,' Eve says, sounding completely un-OK about the whole bedroom invasion.

'We were just – er – wondering about what happened in the cave,' I say, perching down on the edge of her bed.

Eve stiffens. 'What do you mean?'

'About the rock. About how it moved. But it's OK. If – you know – you had something to do with it.'

'We have a secret too,' Holly says quickly.

Eve turns round and stares at us. 'What do you mean, you have a secret?' she says in a tight little voice.

'I'm an energy harnesser and Nessa's an empath. Look.' Holly focuses her attention on the fairy lights strung around the mirror on Eve's dressing table. They start flickering on and off. 'I can do other stuff too – bigger stuff,' Holly says, 'but I didn't want to frighten you – or blow up your bedroom!'

Eve's mouth falls open. I quickly tune in to her feelings and I'm hit by a wall of anger.

'Get out!' she says, taking a step towards us. 'Get out now!'

'What's wrong?' Holly says, looking genuinely shocked. 'We thought you'd be happy.'

'Happy?' Eve's eyes are as wide as saucers. 'Why would I be happy?'

'That you're not the only one,' I say.

'The only what?'

'Witch,' Holly mumbles.

'I don't know what you're talking about,' Eve says. She marches over to the door and flings it open. 'If this is some kind of sick joke I'm really not in the mood. It's bad enough having to put up with this kind of stuff in school but this is my house.'

'I'm so sorry,' I say, walking over to her and touching her on the arm. I'm instantly filled with terror and I hear a voice screaming – screaming, 'George!' Then I feel a wave of guilt. Eve shakes my hand off as if it's scalding. I take a step back and lean against the wall for support as the feeling fades. What on earth just happened?

'We didn't mean to upset you,' Holly says.

'Well, you have,' Eve shouts. 'Now can you please go?'

'Is everything all right up there?' Eve's mum calls from downstairs.

I blink hard, trying to get my brain back into focus. We need to go before her mum comes upstairs. I grab Holly's arm. 'Come on.'

We hurry downstairs. I can hear Eve on the landing behind us, watching us go.

'What's going on?' Eve's mum asks when we get to the hall.

'Nothing – we're just leaving,' I say, too embarrassed to make eye contact with her.

'Why is Eve so upset?' her mum calls after us as we race down the garden path.

But we don't answer her. How can we?

7

Holly and I don't say a word to each other until we've turned the corner from Hollow Hill. As soon as we're out of view of the house Holly stops and stares at me in despair. 'We shouldn't have rushed it. We should have tried to be friends with her first.'

'I know.'

Holly sighs. 'I was just so worried about the Blood Witches.'

'Me too.'

'Do you think they've already told her?'

'I don't know.' I bend over slightly and take a deep breath. I'm still feeling disorientated from what I felt when I touched Eve's arm.

Holly looks at me, concerned. 'Are you OK?'

'Yes. I got one of those flashback things, when we were in Eve's room, when I touched her arm. It's made me feel a bit dizzy and weird.'

Holly puts her hand on my back. 'What was it? What did you see?'

'I didn't really *see* anything. It was more a feeling. I was terrified. And guilty. And I heard someone screaming the name George.'

'Eve's granddad?'

'Yeah. I guess.'

Holly frowns. 'I wonder what that was all about.'

'I don't know.' I sigh. 'But, whatever it is, I feel like we've really blown our chances of finding out.'

Holly shrugs. 'You never know, maybe tomorrow in school things will be better. Maybe once Eve's had a chance to think about what we said she'll be relieved to know she's not alone.'

'But what if we got it all wrong? What if she isn't a witch at all?' My insides start crawling with embarrassment. 'It looks as if we just went round there to pick on her.'

'It looks as if we're *crazy*,' Holly says. 'But that rock didn't move itself. And think of how Izzy and the others were acting towards Eve once we got out of the cave. If we're wrong, then they are too.'

We start slowly making our way along the road, the setting sun glowing red in the sky.

'We're going to have to try to make it up to her in school tomorrow,' I say. 'We can't leave it like this.'

'Don't worry.' Holly links her arm in mine. 'We're the Silver Witches. We'll sort it.'

The next day, as I walk up the long gravel driveway to school, I can't help but feel hopeful as I see the clusters of crocuses dotted like splashes of bright paint in the grass. The spring sunshine is making everything look fresh and new. But then I see Eve. She's standing huddled under a tree in her thick winter coat despite the warmth of the sun. She's obviously waiting until the last possible minute to go into registration. I feel horrible as I realise that Holly and I probably did this to her. I want to go over and apologise but I'm scared I'll make it worse. I decide to wait until I'm with Holly and hurry along the driveway.

The first lesson of the day is Geography with Mr Groddle – or the fascist dictator as Holly calls him. As soon as Eve walks in Izzy calls to her.

'Hey, Eve, come and sit with us.'

Holly and I watch as she trudges to the back of the class where they sit.

'Crap!' Holly mutters.

'Silence!' Mr Groddle barks, causing Holly to drop her pen. 'Today we will be studying rock formations. Turn to page one hundred and eighty-five in your books.' Everything Mr Groddle says is delivered like an insult. Even when he tells us a simple page number it's like he's really saying, *I hate you stupid kids.*

'Is there a problem, Miss Hart?' Mr Groddle

glares at Eve, who's shuffling through her bag, face burning.

'I – I think I've forgotten my book,' Eve stammers.

'You think you have or you have?' Mr Groddle snaps.

'I have.' Eve's voice is barely more than a whisper.

Mr Groddle peers over the rim of his glasses. 'What's that?'

'I have,' Eve says, slightly louder.

I pick my own book up, ready to offer it to her.

'It's OK, sir,' Izzy purrs. 'Eve can share with me.'

I put my book down.

Mr Groddle sighs, like he's disappointed he won't have a reason to keep on shouting. 'Well, all right.' He starts looking at his notes, then turns back to Eve. 'But don't let it happen again!' he yells.

Eve nods. Her eyes are wide with fear behind her glasses. Izzy moves her textbook over to her and Eve manages a small smile.

'Great,' I whisper to Holly.

'Don't worry,' she whispers back. 'There's always lunchtime.'

But at lunchtime Eve walks into the canteen surrounded by Izzy, Vivien and Stephen all giggling and chatting to her like they're her entourage.

'How can she not see that something's up?' Holly says, stabbing at the lid of her yoghurt in despair. 'They've made her life a misery for months. How can she want to hang out with them now?'

I think back to when I first started at Fairhollow High and how Izzy and the others had been all over me. I hadn't realised back then that it was because they thought I might be a witch. That they were being fake with me just like they are now with Eve. I watch Eve as she sits down at the table across from us. Although Izzy and the others are all smiling and laughing, Eve's frowning and she keeps pushing her glasses up against the bridge of her nose, like she's nervous.

'She doesn't exactly look happy about it,' I say

to Holly as I open my lunch box. Aunt Clara's given me some of the leftovers from last night's dinner. A butternut squash couscous salad – one of my favourites. As I take a mouthful I look up and see Izzy staring over at me. It's a look of pure hatred and spite. The flavour drains from my food and my mouth goes dry. I try picturing the door in my mind and slamming it shut but somehow Izzy's feelings are seeping underneath. I start feeling really sick.

'Would it be OK if we have lunch somewhere else?' I say to Holly.

She looks at me, eyebrows raised. 'Of course. Why? What's up?'

I nod slightly in the direction of Izzy. 'I seem to be picking up on her emotions and it's making me feel sick.'

'Oh no.' Holly gets to her feet. 'Come on. Let's go to the library.'

I shove my lunch box back in my bag and stand up.

'Off already?' Izzy calls out. 'What's wrong?

Did you lose your appetite along with your fashion sense?' They all start falling around laughing and it's like someone's cranked up the volume in the canteen to maximum. Every clink of cutlery, every scraping chair, every cackle from Izzy makes my stomach churn and my skin crawl.

Holly puts her arm round my shoulders and gently steers me towards the door. 'Come on,' she whispers in my ear. 'Let's go outside. You'll feel much better once we get away from her.'

'Ha, what a pair of losers,' Stephen calls out.

'You're so weird,' Vivien sneers as we walk past.

You're so weird. You're so weird. You're so weird. Her words ricochet around my head. All I can think about and focus on is getting out of there.

Holly leads me straight to the fire exit at the end of the corridor. I stumble down the steps, gulping in deep breaths of fresh air until, slowly, the pounding in my head starts to fade.

'I hate them!' Holly says pacing up and down. 'They're going to worm their way in with Eve and then they're going to get her to join their pente and then . . .' She breaks off and stares at me. 'Then they'll be only one away from total power and we'll be only one step away from losing our powers completely.'

I lean against the wall, my body filling with a sickness and dread that this time is all mine.

8

'I'm so sorry,' Aunt Clara looks at me mournfully from behind the cash register, 'but would you mind doing the Shelving Job of Doom?'

I start to laugh. 'Of course not.'

'I promise I'll make it up to you,' Aunt Clara says. 'I'll make you all the beetroot brownies you can eat.'

There would have been a time when I'd have seen a promise of beetroot brownies as some kind of threat but now it has me drooling. 'You're on.'

I make my way into the first alcove of books and start scanning the shelves.

It's Saturday and as usual, I'm helping Aunt Clara in the bookshop. The Shelving Job of Doom is when we have to search the entire shop for books that have been put back on the wrong shelf by customers. Normally I hate it but today I'm glad of the chance to do something monotonous. It will help me to think better.

The past week in school has been like watching some cheesy TV show starring Izzy, Vivien and Stephen, called *Sucking Up to Eve*. And Eve has been going out of her way to avoid us. She won't even make eye contact. Every time she looks away it makes me cringe as I think back to how we went round to her house and how weird we must have seemed. I wonder if she told Izzy and the others. I picture them all laughing at us and my stomach churns. I'm so glad to be away from them for a while. Hopefully it will give me the chance to come up with a way to stop them.

I spot a Buddhist book lurking in the astrology section and feel a stab of satisfaction. That's how bad my week's been. I'm actually pleased when I see a wrongly shelved book. I hear the bell above the door jingle. The first customer of the day. I hear the low murmur of a male voice saying something to Aunt Clara and carry on scanning the shelves. There are so many books about astrology. Who knew?

'Nessa!' Aunt Clara calls. 'Could you come and help a customer, please?'

I sigh. Just when I was getting into my Shelving Job of Doom flow. But when I come out of the alcove and see who the customer is my heart skips a beat. Niall. He turns to look at me and grins. When Ellie, my best friend from home, saw him playing in the band at Aunt Clara's New Year's Eve party she instantly named Niall Mr Seriously-Cute-With-a-Capital-C and the title still sticks. His wavy black hair is tied back, making his cheekbones look even more pronounced, and he's wearing his usual musician's attire of faded jeans, scuffed boots and a wrist full of leather bands.

'Hey,' he says softly, as I walk towards him.

Aunt Clara gives me a knowing wink. She thinks

Niall likes me because one time when we were in The Cup and Saucer where he works, he gave me a free dessert. But she doesn't know that when it comes to Niall I have a serious case of Foot-in-Mouth disease.

'Yeah,' I say, trying to sound casual but sounding rude instead. Case proven.

'Could you show Niall the travel section?' Aunt Clara says, now giving me a knowing grin.

'I'm looking for books on Asia,' Niall says.

'Right,' I say, and my face starts burning up, like I find the whole subject of Asia deeply embarrassing. I quickly turn away so he won't see. 'Follow me, please.' Oh God, now I sound like a bossy tour guide.

'I'm thinking of going there in the summer,' Niall says behind me.

'That's great,' I say, this time with way too much enthusiasm, like I'm being sarcastic. Oh, what is wrong with me? 'Here you are,' I say, waving my arm at the travel section. 'Enjoy.'

'Thanks.' Niall walks past me, into the alcove.

I breathe a sigh of relief, tinged with regret.

He turns back to face me. 'Have you ever been to Asia?'

For some reason an image of Niall and me lying in a hammock pops into my mind. He's playing his fiddle and I'm playing my guitar. It's a very big hammock.

'No!' I say firmly, trying to push the image from my mind.

'It looks awesome. I can't decide whether to go to India or Thailand. Maybe I'll do both.'

Now I see a picture of us in a rickshaw. Once again we're playing our instruments, like we're starring in an extremely bad Bollywood movie. What is wrong with my daydreams? Why do they have to be so naff? Niall grins at me. Damn his seriously cute dimply smile. I have books to sort.

'Yes, well, I hope you'll be very happy there.'

Seriously?!

His grin grows, as does his cuteness, like they're

linked by some scientific law. 'Are you OK?' he says.

'Yes. Yes, I'm fine.' I take a deep breath and wrack my brains for something normal to say. 'So, what made you want to go to Asia?' That's more like it.

'My older brother is out there volunteering on his gap year. I'm hoping my parents will let me go and join him afterwards for a couple of weeks. Did you know, in Thailand they have these amazing beach parties at every full moon?'

I shake my head.

'Travellers come from all over the world to do it.' He looks off dreamily.

'Sounds great,' I say, picturing us playing our instruments under a huge full moon.

The bell on the door jangles and I turn round – and see a sight that makes my heart stop. Eve's mum is coming into the shop, pulling a wheelchair through the door.

'I have to go,' I say. 'Bye.'

Niall looks at me, surprised. 'Oh . . . OK.'

I rush to the café at the back of the shop. Aunt Clara is behind the counter, plating up a fresh batch of veggie quiches.

'Is everything OK?' she asks.

'Yes. No. I'll explain later. I just need to take a break for a moment. I'll be right back.'

'Oh . . . OK,' she says, in exactly the same baffled way as Niall.

I rush into the kitchen and lean against the wall. Phew! And there was me thinking that working in the shop was going to be a welcome break from all the dramas at school! What if Eve told her mum what happened the other day – the things we said to her? What if she's come here to complain to Aunt Clara or to have it out with me? Oh my God, what if she has a go at me for invading her daughter's bedroom and talking like a crazy person *in front of Niall*!

'Good morning!' I hear Aunt Clara call. 'Can I help you?'

'Morning,' I hear Eve's mum say. I hold my

breath. 'Could we get some drinks to take out, please?'

I relax a fraction. I wonder if Eve is with them.

'Of course,' Aunt Clara replies. 'What would you like?'

'Could I have a peppermint tea, please?' Eve's mum says. 'And what would you like, George?'

'Orange juice, please,' I hear a young guy say. I hold my breath. He definitely sounded young, not at all like a granddad-aged old man.

'And I'll have a ginger tea, please,' a man's voice says. I guess he must be Eve's dad.

'Of course.' I hear Aunt Clara getting some take-away cups from the shelf behind the counter. Eve can't be with them. I breathe a sigh of relief.

'I tell you what, why don't George and I go and get our football magazines while you get the drinks?' Eve's dad says. 'We'll meet you outside the newsagent's.'

'OK,' Eve's mum replies.

I hear the sound of George and his dad's voices

drifting off down the shop and a few seconds later the bell above the door jangles.

'You're the Harts, aren't you?' Aunt Clara says. There's a hiss of steam as she makes one of the drinks.

'Yes, that's right,' Eve's mum replies.

'I knew your grandmother,' Aunt Clara says. 'Elizabeth. She was great friends with my grandma.'

'Really?' Eve's mum sounds relaxed, happy even. I breathe another sigh of relief. Eve can't have told her what happened. Or at least, she can't have told her my name or that I'm related to Aunt Clara.

'Yes. You look very like her, you know.'

Eve's mum laughs. 'That's what everyone's been saying, since we moved back here. It's nice though. I didn't really know her all that well. My parents moved away from Fairhollow when I was little and I think I only saw her a handful of times before she died, so my memories of her are very hazy.'

'She was a lovely woman,' Aunt Clara says. 'My grandma used to talk of her so fondly.'

'Ah, that's nice to hear.'

'So, what brought you back here?' Aunt Clara asks and I hear another hiss from the hot-water heater.

'Well, after what happened to George, we really needed a fresh start and to be closer to the rest of our family.' Eve's mum's voice goes quiet.

'Oh, I'm sorry, I didn't mean to pry,' Aunt Clara says quickly.

'No, it's fine. It's not as if it's a secret.'

I turn to face the door to the café and focus all of my attention on Aunt Clara. *Ask her what happened*, I will her. *Ask her what happened to George.*

'Here's your tea,' Aunt Clara says and for a moment I wonder if my empath abilities have failed.

'I think I have the right money,' Eve's mum says.

Ask her what happened to George. I picture the thought burrowing its way into Aunt Clara's brain.

'Do you mind me asking how it happened?' Aunt Clara asks softly.

Yes! I lean back against the wall, relieved.

'No, not at all. It was a car accident, one of those freak accidents, actually. You know, the kind you read about sometimes in the papers, with no real explanation. We were on our way to a caravan holiday. Everything was so normal. Bill, my husband was singing along to the radio. Eve was in a sulk about something or other, and then suddenly one of those huge telecom poles just crashed down on to the car and crushed George's legs. The rest of us all walked away unscathed. Well, physically, at least. I think the whole thing's really scarred Eve – my daughter. She was in the back with him. She saw it close up. It could so easily have happened to her.'

'I'm so sorry,' says Aunt Clara.

'Thank you. It certainly has been a tough time. The doctors aren't sure he'll ever walk again.'

I hear the rustle of a paper bag.

'Here, take these brownies,' Aunt Clara says. 'For you and the children. On the house.'

'Oh no, I couldn't.'

'Yes, I insist. And you can have the drinks free too.'

'No, really, I wasn't saying all of that to get –'

'I know you weren't,' Aunt Clara interrupts. 'I want to do it. And it's what our grandmothers would have wanted too.'

Eve's mum laughs. 'That's so lovely of you. Thank you.'

'You're very welcome. Hope to see you in here again soon.'

'Oh, you will,' Eve's mum says.

As they say goodbye I take a deep breath and sort through this latest revelation. This accident must have been what I picked up on in Eve's bedroom. The terror she felt when the pole came crashing down. The sound of her voice screaming, 'George'. But why did I feel guilty? Why did *Eve* feel guilty?

I get the overwhelming urge to see Holly to tell her what's happened but she's away with her parents for the weekend.

'Hey, Clara, could I pay for this, please?' The sound of Niall's voice jolts me back to reality.

'Of course,' Aunt Clara replies. 'So you're off to Thailand then, are you?'

'I hope so.'

I feel a pang of sorrow and immediately tell myself off for being so sappy. I've got way more important things to worry about right now than Niall dancing under a full moon in Thailand.

'Oh, could I ask you a favour too?' Niall asks.

'Yes of course,' Aunt Clara replies.

'Blue Harbour are looking for a new guitarist. Would it be OK to leave these flyers about the auditions on the counter?'

I feel a shiver of excitement as I remember Blue Harbour playing in Paper Soul on New Year's Eve and how I played guitar with them for one song. It had gone really well. An image of Niall and me playing together in the band flashes into my mind and – unlike my hammock and rickshaw and full moon beach party daydreams – this one actually feels achievable.

9

On Monday I walk into the classroom feeling determined that this week is going to be better than last. Having two days away from Izzy, Vivien and Stephen has helped me feel stronger. There's no sign of them in the classroom yet – or Eve – but Holly is sitting at our usual table, her nose stuck in a book. I hurry over, plonk my bag on the floor and sit down.

'Oh, it's so good to see you!' she exclaims, snapping her book shut. 'I've had the weekend from hell with my parents.'

'You didn't blow up the hotel, did you?' I say with a smile. Holly's had a few mishaps with electrical appliances since she got her energy-harnessing power.

'No. But I wish I had. At least something interesting would have happened. I don't know why they had to drag me along with them. All they did was drone on about work. Svetlana's dad better hurry up and get better soon.'

Svetlana is Holly's au pair. Her dad had a heart attack a few weeks ago so she's gone back to Russia to be with him.

'Anyway, what was it you needed to tell me?'

I'd texted Holly on Saturday to let her know I had something important to tell her. I didn't want to text about Eve in case Holly's parents checked her phone. I glance around the classroom. Other students are filing in but there's still no sign of Izzy, Vivien and Stephen, or Eve.

'Eve's mum came into the café at Paper Soul on Saturday,' I whisper.

Holly's eyes widen. 'No way! What did she say? Did she tell Aunt Clara about us coming to their house? Did she shout at you?'

I shake my head. 'No, she just came in for some drinks. I managed to escape to the kitchen without her seeing me and I don't think she knows I'm related to Aunt Clara. Anyway, guess what? George isn't Eve's granddad – he's her brother.'

'Her brother? But – why does he need a stairlift?'

'He was injured in a car accident.'

'How do you know?'

'I made Aunt Clara ask her.'

Holly frowns. 'You made her? How?'

'With my empath power.'

'No way!' Holly looks really excited. 'You know what this means?'

'What?'

'You won't need to text me any more. You can just send messages straight to my brain!'

'I don't think I'm that good yet to be honest. But anyway, that isn't all that happened – you'll never guess what Eve's mum told Aunt Clara.'

'What?' Holly practically yells, causing some

of our classmates to stare at us.

'Shhh!' I huddle closer to her. 'They were in a freak accident in their car. One of those huge telephone poles crashed down on them.'

'You're kidding?'

'No. Apparently they were on their way to a holiday and everything was totally normal. Eve's dad was singing and Eve was sulking about something and then this pole just crashed down on them completely out of the blue. No wonder I felt so scared when I got the flashback – it must have been terrifying.'

Holly nods. Then she frowns. 'Hang on, what did you just say about Eve?'

'She was in a car accident.'

'No, the bit about when she was in the car?'

'She was singing. Oh no, that was her dad. She was sulking.'

'Right. She was sulking and then bang, a pole drops on them out of nowhere.'

'What are you saying?'

'I'm saying, what if she is telekinetic and she made the pole fall down?'

I stare at Holly. 'What, on purpose?'

'No! But you know what it's like when your powers first come through. You know how hard it is to control them. Look at how many appliances I've blown up. And what about that time at the school dance when you made Izzy fall over?'

I nod. 'And that time you made the lamppost blow just by leaning on it.'

'Exactly. What if the same thing happened to Eve? She could have just been starting to get her power. Maybe she didn't even realise what it was or how to control it.'

'*Eve was in a sulk about something or other.*' Eve's mum's words echo through my mind, causing a chill to run up my spine. Did Eve accidentally cause the pole to crash down on the car because of her bad mood? And then another piece of the jigsaw falls into place.

'That would explain why she feels guilty too.

Do you remember, when I had the flashback, I felt her guilt as well as her terror?'

'Wow!' Holly shakes her head. 'If that is what happened, she's got one crazy power.'

'I know. And just think what will happen if she joins the Blood Witches – how much damage she could cause.'

At exactly that moment, Eve shuffles through the door, head down. She looks so timid and shy it seems crazy to think she's capable of causing huge poles to come crashing down and rocks to move.

'And if she did cause the accident,' Holly says, unaware that Eve is right behind her, 'if she did do that to her brother, she must feel horrible.'

I see Eve recoil before hurrying over to the table furthest away.

'I think she heard you,' I hiss at Holly.

Holly gasps and looks over her shoulder at Eve. Eve glares back at her before turning away. 'She hates us,' Holly says mournfully.

*

At lunchtime, Holly and I decide to skip going to the canteen and eat our sandwiches out on the field. I'd been feeling a weird uneasiness in lessons all morning and assumed it was to do with being around Izzy. But, as we sit under a tree, the feeling grows.

'Are you ...? Is everything OK?' I ask, wondering if I'm picking up something from Holly.

'Yes, I'm fine,' she replies, unwrapping her sausage rolls.

I reach into my bag for my lunch and see one of the flyers about the band auditions Niall left in the shop. I'd brought it in to show Holly.

'Look at this,' I say, handing it to her.

She scans the words.

'I'm going to try out.'

'Oh, wow, that's so cool,' she says, her brown eyes shining.

'It's – er – the band that Niall plays for. You know, the guy from The Cup and Saucer.'

Holly's smile instantly fades. 'Oh.' She hands the

flyer back to me and takes a bite of her sausage roll.

'What's wrong?'

'Nothing.' But she can't even look at me.

'I thought you'd be happy for me. You know how much I love playing the guitar.'

'Yeah, and I know how much you love Niall.' Holly sounds really bitter.

'What? Why are you being like this?' I study her face. It's so weird for Holly to be like this. Could it be that she's jealous?

'How much do you know about him, Nessa?'

I shrug. 'Not a lot. He's in Year Ten. He goes to Newbridge High. He wants to go to Thailand on holiday. Why?'

'I don't know.' Holly starts picking at the grass. 'There's something about him I'm not sure of.'

'What?'

'I don't know. You're the empath. Have you ever picked up anything about him?'

I shake my head. I get another strong feeling of unease and this time I'm certain it's coming from

Holly. I can practically see it rolling off her in waves.

'What's the matter, Holl? I know you're stressing about something. I can feel it.'

Holly gives a dramatic sigh. 'Oh, the joys of being friends with an empath!'

We both laugh.

'It's Svetlana,' she says eventually. 'Her dad's taken a turn for the worse so she won't be coming back this week. I got a text from my mum while we were in Maths. She's saying I might have to go away with her and Dad next week. They've got a big case starting in London.'

'No way!'

'Yes way. My life sucks.'

I put the flyer back in my bag. That must be why Holly got so weird about Niall. She's stressing about her parents. I feel a weird mixture of sadness and relief. Relief that at least she isn't jealous, but sadness that she might have to go away again.

10

Usually, Music is my favourite lesson but not now Izzy, Vivien and Stephen have turned it into a particularly cringey episode of *Suck Up to Eve*.

'OMG, you're such an amazing flute player!' Izzy gushes as Eve practically deafens us with a piercing toot.

'Flautist,' Holly mutters as she taps unenthusiastically on a tambourine.

'What?' Izzy says icily.

'She's such an amazing *flautist*,' Holly repeats, louder this time. 'It's the proper name for a flute player. Like guitarist.'

'Yeah, right,' Stephen says with a mocking laugh.

'Then why's it called a flute not a flaut?' He hits the xylophone in front of him tunelessly.

Eve's face flushes and she puts the flute down.

'Keep playing, Eve,' Izzy says gently. 'Don't let them put you off.'

'How are we putting her off?' Holly says indignantly.

'Go on, you're really good,' Izzy says encouragingly.

Eve smiles at Izzy.

'Leave it,' I mutter to Holly. Izzy seems to be able to twist everything we say into something bad.

'OK, does everyone have an instrument?' the Music teacher, Mr Graham, asks as he comes back into the classroom, shutting the cupboard door behind him.

'Can I swap the xylophone for the bongos, sir?' Stephen calls.

'No, Stephen. We need to get on with the lesson.' Mr Graham starts handing out sheets of music. 'The bongos are right at the back of the cupboard.'

'No, they're not, sir,' Stephen says smugly. 'They're right here.'

I turn and see the bongos on the table in front of Stephen. I look at Holly.

'Ghosting,' we both whisper as we work out what's gone on.

'What? But I thought . . .' Mr Graham scratches his head in disbelief. 'I could have sworn the bongos were still in the cupboard.'

Vivien gets up and walks over to our table. My whole body tenses as she picks up a recorder, then bends down as if she's fiddling with her shoe. 'You must be getting old and senile, sir,' she says. But she says it in my voice. I instinctively shove her away from me and she goes toppling over on to her side.

'Nessa!' Mr Graham exclaims. 'And I'm not sure what triggered that violent outburst but I suggest you give it some serious thought in detention this afternoon.'

'But, sir . . .' I see Eve staring at me, horrified, and I feel sick. She must think I'm a lunatic.

'But nothing. Now, can we please get on with the lesson?'

As the world's worst version of 'Greensleeves' starts booming around the classroom I feel furious at the injustice of it all. How is it fair that the Blood Witches can get away with this and us Silver Witches aren't able to retaliate because we have to use our powers for good? It's already bad enough that they're only two away from forming their pente – one if Eve joins them. As the crashing noise from our Music lesson gets louder so do my fears.

'Don't worry,' Holly whispers in my ear. 'You can still come round to mine after your detention, to work on our powers. I'm sure it won't be long now before I can make fire from nothing.'

'I won't be able to come to yours now I've got a detention,' I whisper back. 'I'll need to go straight home and practise for the audition.'

Holly's face falls and she bangs hard on her tambourine. Great, now I've upset my best friend. Can today get any worse?

*

When I get to the detention room at the end of the day I'm surprised to see Eve sitting there.

'Hey,' I say as I sit down at a desk next to hers.

She nods. 'Hey.'

At least she isn't completely blanking me.

'What are you here for?' I ask.

'Skipping PE,' she mutters. 'I hate PE.'

'Me too,' I say quickly, even though it isn't really true. At this point I think I'd say or do anything to get Eve to trust me and not think of me as some kind of psycho.

The teacher comes in and we both take our homework folders from our bags.

I stare down at my half-written History essay but it might as well be written in Japanese. All I can think about is Eve. I need to read her feelings, see if I can pick up anything. I close my eyes and focus all of my attention in her direction. I picture a giant door swinging open in my mind. I feel a sense of peace, almost happiness. It's totally different to how

Eve was feeling on the school trip. My heart sinks as I work out why. It must be her friendship with Izzy and the others. I remember how grateful I was when they first befriended me – before I realised that they were a bunch of evil fakes. Eve's spent so long on her own at school, no wonder she's happy. But what can I do? I can hardly try telling her the truth. Not after what happened last time.

I take a deep breath and see if I can pick up anything about Eve wanting to become a Blood Witch. But all I get is a sweet softness. That's something at least. Eve might be happy that she's friends with Izzy, Vivien and Stephen. But it doesn't seem that they've revealed themselves to her yet. Hopefully she'd feel very different if she knew the truth behind their phoney attempts at friendship.

11

Are you free to chat lol

As I look down at the text from my dad I can't help smiling. No matter how many times I tell him lol means laugh out loud, he still thinks it means lots of love.

Yes! Just about to go out but if you call me now you can come with me lol

I hoist my guitar case over my shoulder, shut the shop door behind me and start walking up the High Street. The air outside feels sticky and humid, like a storm's brewing. I look up at the sky. It's a weird yellowy shade of white. My phone starts playing 'Hey Jude', the ringtone I have just for my dad. It's his favourite song. I answer it within a second.

'Hey, Dad.'

'Hello!' Dad says, his voice faint and slightly crackly.

I push down the wistful pang I feel as I think of how long it's been since I've seen him.

'So, how's your week going?' he says.

'Great. I'm just off to an audition.'

'Sorry – you cut out a bit there. An auction? What for?'

'No, an audition,' I say loudly, causing a passing woman to stare at me. 'For a band.'

There's a couple of seconds' silence and I can't work out if it's the time delay or I've shocked him into silence.

'That's fantastic!' Dad cries, his voice crystal clear this time. 'What kind of band?'

'A mix of folk and rock. You'd love them. They're the band I played a song with on New Year's Eve.

The ones who were playing at Aunt Clara's party. Do you remember me telling you?'

'Of course I do.' There's a moment's silence. 'You played "Hey Jude", didn't you? I only wish I could have seen you.'

I feel another pang of sorrow. 'Me too. I miss you, Dad.'

'I miss you too, Ness.'

'But if I get into the band you'll be able to see me play when you're home on leave.'

I cross over a side road and continue up the High Street, past the greengrocer who's busy packing away his crates of fruit and veg.

'That would be great,' Dad says, sounding happy again. 'Did I ever tell you that I was in a band?'

'No! When?'

'When I was in high school. We were called Malcolm and the Muppets. I was one of the Muppets.' He starts to laugh.

'No way!' I think of the teenage Dad I've seen

in photos, with his long hair and weird clothes, playing his electric guitar in a band. 'That's amazing.'

'Yeah, it was, until Malcolm decided he wanted to be an actor instead of lead singer and one of the Muppets had to give up due to his commitments with the boy scouts. Rock and roll, man.'

As I start to laugh my body fills with warmth. It feels so great joking with Dad like this, like the good old days of me and him in our London life. Then I see the music store up ahead and feel a burst of nerves.

'OK, Dad, I'm going to have to go, I'm almost at the audition venue.'

'Already? That was quick!'

'Yeah well, that's small-town life. It only takes about five minutes to get anywhere.'

'Ha, opposite to London, then.'

'Yep, opposite to London.' But as I say this I don't feel as homesick as I used to. I walk up to the music store. The lights in the window are out but

I can see some people milling about in the back.

'OK, here goes,' I say, pushing the door open. 'Wish me luck.'

'Good luck, Ness,' Dad says. 'Knock 'em dead.'

As I make my way to the back of the store I feel nervous but happy. Speaking to Dad has made me feel as if he's still here with me somehow. And it's been so nice to talk about something normal for once. It makes me glad that Dad doesn't know I'm a witch. My warm glow fizzles out the second I see Vivien. She's sitting in one of the chairs that have been arranged in a semi-circle around what I guess must be the performing space. She's deep in conversation with a dark-haired guy sitting next to her. He's holding a guitar. There's a Goth girl about Niall's age with long wine-red hair sitting next to them, tightening the strings on her guitar. And next to her there's a boy I recognise from the year above in school and he's chatting to Niall.

'Hello! I'm Daniel.' A guy comes bounding over holding a battered notebook and pen. I recognise him immediately as the lead singer from the band. 'Are you here for the audition?'

I nod, unable to say anything, unable to think anything apart from, *Why is Vivien here?*

'Can I take your name, please?' Daniel says.

'My what?' I look back at him.

'Your name?'

'Oh yes, sorry. Nessa.' How can Vivien be trying out for the band? I've never seen her playing guitar before in Music.

Daniel frowns. 'Wait a minute, don't I know you from somewhere?'

I nod. 'Yes. I played with you guys at my aunt's New Year's Eve party.'

His eyes light up. 'You're Clara's niece?'

'Yes.'

'I remember. You were great! OK, I just need to take a few more details. How old are you?'

'Thirteen.' As I say it, it sounds so young. I hope it won't matter.

'Really? Wow, you look older. OK, great.' Daniel

gestures to the semi-circle of chairs. 'Take a seat. We're about to begin.'

The only empty seats are next to Vivien or at the other side of the semi-circle next to Niall. I head over to Niall. Vivien looks up and as she notices me I feel hatred seeping like an icy fog across the room. I quickly block it out. There's no way I'm going to let her put me off my audition.

'Oh, hey, Nessa,' Niall says, turning to face me. 'I was hoping you'd be here.'

'You were?'

'Yeah. I was going to ask you to come on Saturday, in the shop, before you did your disappearing act.'

'Yeah, uh, sorry about that. I had something I needed to do in the kitchen – uh – urgently.' Oh God, shoot me now.

But thankfully, before I can make myself look any more stupid, Daniel comes and stands in front of us.

'Thanks so much for coming, guys,' he says. 'Let's crack on with the auditions.' He looks at his notepad. 'First up, could we have Marcus Daglish please?'

The dark-haired guy next to Vivien gets to his feet and she hands him the guitar. It all falls into place. Daglish is Vivien's surname. He must be her brother. And now he's standing in front of me I can definitely see the family resemblance. He has the same long nose and square jaw. I breathe a sigh of relief. Vivien must have come along to give him support. Although the thought of Vivien supporting anyone is totally laughable.

'Is it all right if I sing as well?' Marcus asks Daniel. 'I mean, I know you're, like, the lead singer, but, you know, in case you ever want me to do some backing vocals.'

'Sure,' Daniel says, sitting down next to me. 'Go for it.'

As Marcus starts strumming his guitar a terrible thought occurs to me. What if he's a Blood Witch too?

Marcus starts singing – or it could be howling

111

– there's really no way to tell. I grit my teeth and resist the urge to cover my ears. If he is a witch, there's no way he's a mimic. If you could pick any voice in the world, why would you choose to sound like a cat being strangled? His guitar-playing isn't any better either. It's like he's way more concerned with how he looks than how he sounds as he throws his head back and strums mindlessly at the strings.

I see Daniel glance across me at Niall, then look at their other bandmates, who are standing by the wall. He doesn't look impressed. None of them do. But what if Marcus has some other kind of power? Then I remember Aunt Clara telling Holly and me everything she knew about the Blood Witches' families. Vivien's father wasn't a witch. He left them when Vivien was just a little girl. And the witch gene can only be passed through the same sex. I breathe a sigh of relief and look at Vivien. She's looking down at the floor. Could it be that she's actually embarrassed?

Marcus's audition finally comes to an end. My ears are still ringing though.

'OK. Thank you, Marcus,' Daniel says. 'That was definitely . . . different.'

Definitely different. One of the best cop-out answers ever.

I feel a pang of nerves as Daniel looks at his notebook. 'Next up, can we have John Wilkinson, please?'

'Go on, Jonno!' Niall cries, patting the guy next to him on the back.

My heart sinks. He's Niall's friend. Surely Niall will want him in the band more than anyone else?

As John starts to play, I feel a pinprick of hope. He's definitely better than Marcus – though let's face it, a pneumatic drill would be better than Marcus – but there's something missing. I'm not sure what it is. He just seems to play it too safe. There's no spark. No X factor.

Next, Daniel calls the girl with the long burgundy hair. Her name is Violet, which sounds a bit like an old lady's name to me but she plays beautifully. Unlike the previous two, you can tell she really loves playing. I'm about to feel disheartened but then I think of my dad and I remember what he said to me. All I can do is play my best and enjoy every moment of it.

When Daniel calls my name everything goes weirdly numb. I go and stand in front of the chairs but it's like I've edited the others into a soft haze. The only thing that's in focus is my guitar. I start playing and for the first few chords I feel stiff and self-conscious but then, as always, the music lifts me up and I'm carried on its current, like a bird in a jet stream. It doesn't matter that Vivien is watching me. If anything all of the pent-up feelings and emotions of the past couple of weeks are now fuelling my music, coming out through my fingers and into the guitar. My entire body relaxes, bending and swaying in time with the melody as the music builds and builds and then finally it's over. I keep my eyes closed for a second, still lost in the moment, until a burst of applause jolts me from my trance.

'That was awesome,' I hear Daniel say.

I open my eyes and see Niall grinning at me and nodding his head. 'Good job, Nessa,' he says.

I hurry back to my seat, my skin tingling from the music and the applause. I don't even look in Vivien's direction. I don't want anything to ruin this feeling.

'Right,' Daniel says, leaping to his feet. 'My bandmates and I are just going to have a quick chat out back and then hopefully we'll be able to let you know our decision.' He and Niall and the other members of the band head out through a small door at the back of the shop. The rest of us sit in silence.

'I really think I nailed it,' Marcus says to Vivien. He might not have the family witch gene but he definitely has the arrogant one.

As I put my guitar back in its case I slowly come back down from my cloud. I think it went well. It must have gone well, for them all to clap me. But did I do enough? I think of Niall saying 'good job' and how he'd hoped I'd be at the audition. That must mean he'd like me in the band, mustn't it? But he's obviously good friends with John too.

After what feels like an eternity – and even longer than Marcus's audition – the band members return to the shop.

'OK, we've made our decision.' Daniel looks at me and smiles – before turning away. 'Violet, we'd love it if you'd join us.'

I feel a sharp stab of disappointment. And a childish voice in my head says, *But no one clapped her audition.*

Violet starts saying, 'Thank you so much,' over and over and over again. Marcus actually huffs and marches out, followed closely by Vivien. And John looks how I feel – totally gutted.

'Sorry, mate,' Niall says, coming over and placing a hand on John's shoulder. 'It was a group decision. There was nothing I could do.'

John shrugs. 'That's OK. Ah well, better get off for football training.'

Niall and I watch John as he trudges to the door.

'Did I – did I do something wrong?' I blurt out.

'No! Of course not. You were great,' Niall says, glancing over to the rest of the band.

I try to tune into to him, to work out how he's feeling but I get nothing. I guess I'm too disappointed to be able to focus properly. 'Can I ask . . .?' I break off, not wanting to sound like a bad loser.

Niall looks back at me, his blue eyes twinkling. 'What?'

'Why wasn't I chosen? I mean, is there something I should be doing differently – or better?'

Niall shakes his head. 'No. It's just that . . . we thought you were a bit too young.'

'Oh.' His words sting. I'm too young. Great. 'OK. Well, I guess I'd better get going, then.'

'OK. See you.' Niall gives me one final grin then bounds off to join the others.

I head to the door, my thoughts a tangled mess of confusion.

The next day, I wake up with a crick in my neck and a dull thumping ache in my head. Even worse, I wake up late for school. In all of my disappointment over the audition I forgot to set my alarm. I leap from the bed, have a ten-second shower, get dressed and race downstairs. Aunt Clara had to get up super-early this morning to go and check out a new supplier of tofu in Edinburgh. But for once, I'm glad she's not here. It was bad enough having to tell her I failed the audition when I got home last night, but there's no way I want to have to talk to her about it again. Ditto my dad. He texted last night to find out how I got on but I couldn't bring myself to put it into writing.

I'm so late for school I miss registration and have to head straight to my first lesson – English. I can hear the noise from my class before I can even see the classroom, which is weird because normally English is one of our quietest lessons – unless Holly hasn't enjoyed the book we've been set, then all hell breaks loose. I open the door to see everyone chatting away animatedly while a very anxious-looking supply teacher sits at the front, tapping her desk with a pen. I head straight over to Holly, the only person in the classroom who's actually reading.

'Hey,' I say, slumping down into the chair next to her.

'Hey.' She snaps her book shut. 'How did the audition go? Why didn't you reply to my text last night?'

'I didn't get chosen for the band. I was too disappointed.'

'Oh no.' Holly looks sympathetic but I feel a spark of happiness coming from her. Why is she happy that I didn't get in? Is it because she doesn't like Niall? I decide to ignore it. Maybe she's happy about something else, like being in English or something. Even though it doesn't exactly look like we're having a lesson today.

'Where's Miss Johnson?' I ask, pulling my copy of our course text from my bag.

'Gretna Green,' Holly replies.

I look at her, shocked. Gretna Green is a small town in Scotland where people run away to get married on the sly. 'What?'

'OK, well "officially" she's off sick with the flu but Mr Graham is off today too.' Holly's eyes shine with excitement. 'I think they're finally doing it. I think they're finally tying the knot.'

I laugh and shake my head. Holly has this crazy notion that Miss Johnson and Mr Graham are wildly in love, all because Miss Johnson once asked him if we could borrow some cymbals for a class reading of *Macbeth* – to crash for the sound of thunder – and he said, 'Yes of course, Lulu.' This use of a pet name equals a total declaration of love in Holly's eyes.

'He might have caught the flu from her, you know?'

Holly's eyes light up even brighter. 'More proof that they're an item!'

'Could everyone please read their copies of *1984*?' the supply teacher nervously calls, before retreating back behind her own copy of the book.

'I hope supply teachers have a support group,' Holly says. 'It's got to be the worst job in the world.'

I hear Vivien laughing loudly and turn to see her, Izzy, Stephen and Eve all looking over in my direction. I wonder if she's telling them about the audition. Then I wonder what lies she must have told them to make them laugh. Suddenly I've had enough of the Blood Witches and their smugness. I look straight into Vivien's eyes and in my head I yell, *SHUT UP!* The smile vanishes from Vivien's face and she quickly looks away.

I feel a surge of satisfaction. My ability to transfer thoughts into another person's mind is obviously getting stronger. And it feels so good to remind Vivien that they're not the only ones with powers.

I turn back to Holly. 'You'll never guess who was at the audition last night.'

'Niall?' Holly says flatly.

'No – well, yes, obviously, but Vivien was there too, with her brother.'

Holly instantly looks more interested. 'What? Why?'

'Her brother was trying out for the band.'

Holly looks horrified. 'He didn't get it, did he?'

'No. He was awful.'

'Please keep the noise down,' the supply teacher says, not even bothering to look out from behind her book this time.

The noise in the classroom fades slightly.

'I have a cousin who had the same injuries as your brother,' I hear Stephen say, over the murmur.

I glance across the room at him. He's talking to Eve – a very shocked-looking Eve.

'How do you know about my brother?' she says.

I nudge Holly and nod my head slightly in their direction to get her to listen.

'Oh, I think I heard it from someone in town,' Stephen says vaguely. 'Anyway, my cousin ended up having surgery in America and now he's walking again.'

Eve's face lights up. 'Really? My parents are trying to find enough money to send George to America, but they've only got about half of what they need. He's on a waiting list for treatment here too.' Her face falls again and she looks down at her desk.

'Oh, how horrible for you.' I cringe as Izzy places her hand on Eve's shoulder. 'It must be so tough.'

Eve nods but seems unable to speak.

'I know,' Vivien says, sounding a little too

enthusiastic. 'Why don't we help your parents raise the rest of the money?'

'What? How?' Eve looks at her blankly.

I see Izzy give Vivien a knowing smirk behind Eve's back. 'That's a great idea,' she says.

What are they up to?

'Yeah,' says Stephen. 'If my family could do it for my cousin then we can definitely do it for your brother.'

'But – but why would you do that?' Eve looks at each of them in shock.

'Oh my God,' Holly hisses in my ear. 'This is horrible.'

'Because you're our friend,' Izzy says, her eyes wide. 'And we'd do anything for our friends. Wouldn't we, guys?'

I turn away feeling sick.

After school, Holly and I head straight to the old oak tree. It feels right that, given the size of the problem we're facing, we should come to the special gathering place of the Silver Witches. I'm hoping that the tree will give us some inspiration about what to do. We sit down in the crook between its huge roots. The ground feels soft and springy beneath my hands. So different from how icy hard it was the first time I came here. I take a deep breath and close my eyes. I think of my mum Celeste and Aunt Clara sitting here when they were our age, with their fellow Silver Witches and I sigh. What if this is it? What if Holly and I are the only Silver Witches of this generation? I turn and look at her.

'What are we going to do?'

Holly shrugs. 'I don't know.'

I start picking at the moss on the ground in frustration. 'If they really are going to help raise money for Eve's brother we've got no chance of convincing her that they're bad news. They'll be heroes.'

I feel little darts of concern coming off Holly and prickling my skin. 'We need to come up with a plan,' she says. 'We need to stop them getting Eve

to join them and we need to do whatever it takes.'
She places her hand over mine. 'Silver forever.'

A jolt runs up my arm, filling me with strength.
'Silver forever,' I reply.

13

'Wow, the amber is really beautiful,' Holly says, taking a crystal pendant from the tray and holding it up to the light. 'It's like a flame inside a stone.'

It's Saturday and, as Aunt Clara doesn't need my help in Paper Soul, we've gone shopping. Saturday shopping with a friend used to mean Ellie and me browsing through make-up and books. Now it means Holly and me browsing through healing crystals, trying to get some extra protection from the Blood Witches. I look at the piece of paper Aunt Clara gave me with tips on which crystals to get.

'Amber's on the list,' I say. 'Apparently it's great for protection.'

'Cool!' Holly wraps her fingers around the amber. 'How about you? Which one are you going to get?'

I look down at the tray and my eyes are drawn to a white stone that's tinged with pale blue. 'I really like this one,' I say, picking it up.

Holly reads the sign on the tray. 'Moonstone. Is that on Clara's list?'

I hold the moonstone up to the light and it shimmers silver and blue. I get the strongest feeling that it's the one for me. I quickly scan Aunt Clara's list. Moonstone is there, right at the bottom. *Great for intuition*, she's written next to it with a smiley face. The perfect stone for an empath – and I knew it before I even read her words. I nod to Holly and grin.

'OK, cool, let's go and pay.'

I follow Holly up to the counter. The jewellery store is like most of the other shops in Fairhollow – old and narrow with lots of wooden beams. When I first came here I found the olde worlde buildings a bit spooky but now I love them. We buy our crystal pendants and silver chains to wear them on.

'Let's put them on now,' Holly says as we walk to the door.

I put my moonstone pendant around my neck. It might be wishful thinking, but I immediately feel stronger. Just as I'm about to open the door I see Izzy, Vivien and Stephen on the High Street outside. 'Wait,' I say to Holly and point through the glass. We watch as they start pinning a poster to the noticeboard across from the shop. We're too far away to be able to read what it says.

'What do you think it's for?' I whisper.

'I don't know.' Holly replies. 'Maybe it's a WANTED poster.' She puts on a TV-announcer-style voice. 'Wanted – kindness and compassion.'

I laugh. 'Yeah. Or a MISSING poster – for Stephen's brain.'

We watch as they move down the High Street, sticking more posters to every available lamppost.

'Well, whatever it is, they definitely want

people to know about it,' Holly mutters.

Once they've gone, we head out of the shop and over to the poster.

'Oh no!' Holly exclaims, as if she's the empath and she's reading my thoughts.

The poster is for a fund-raising fete – *for our dear friend's brother to have vital surgery*, it reads.

'I can't believe they're going this far,' I say. 'I mean, I thought they might offer to donate some money or something, but to put on an entire fete?'

Holly nods. 'It's so unfair. Izzy's so rich and well-connected she can do things like this. She can arrange a fete at the drop of a hat. It's going to make it so much easier for them to complete their pente. If they're always able to go all out like this, how will we be able to stop them?'

An icy shiver courses through my body, from the tips of my toes to the top of my scalp. 'I think we need to tell Aunt Clara.'

Holly nods. 'Yes. We could definitely do with her help.'

'Why don't you come back to mine and stay for dinner? She's always on at me to invite you over.'

'Ha, how times have changed!'

We both laugh. It's so weird thinking that there was a time when Aunt Clara was so desperate to keep me from Holly she was even thinking of making me change school.

'That would be great though,' Holly says. 'Get me away from my parents. I don't think I can handle any more guilt-induced "quality time". I might actually explode. Seriously, sometimes I wish they'd just go away on a work trip and never come back.' She clamps her hand to her mouth. 'Oh my God! I'm so sorry! I didn't mean . . . That was so thoughtless of me.'

I shake my head. 'It's fine. I understand.'

'But your parents – I should have thought.'

'No, really, it's fine. I was so young when Mum died I can't even remember her, let alone miss her. I mean, I miss the idea of her, of course, but her not being here is all I've ever known. And I'm definitely getting used to not seeing my dad. Anyway, I've still got Aunt Clara – and you.'

'Yes, your insensitive friend!'

'You're a great friend.'

Holly looks at me, eyes wide. 'Really?'

'Of course.'

She starts to smile. 'No one's ever said that to me before.' She links arms with me and we start walking back along the High Street towards Paper Soul. 'Let's go and ask Aunt Clara how we can defeat the Blood Witches once and for all.'

I laugh. 'Funny – no one's ever said that to me before either.'

Aunt Clara makes mushroom risotto for dinner, which is one of my favourites but I'm so anxious about telling her what's going on I've lost my appetite. I play with my fork, wondering how best to say it.

'Is everything OK, Nessa?' Aunt Clara asks, looking across the kitchen table at me. The candles flicker, casting shadows on her scarlet hair.

'Yes, I'm fine,' I say.

She frowns and raises one of her thin, dark eyebrows. 'Really? You can't kid an empath, you know. My powers might be dimming but I still know another person's anxiety when I feel it.'

'Huh, welcome to my world,' Holly says with a sigh. 'I mean, I think your power's really cool and everything but sometimes it can be a little annoying hanging out with a couple of mind readers.'

Aunt Clara and I both laugh, then she looks back at me. 'Seriously, though. What's wrong?'

'It's Izzy and the others,' I say.

'I should have known.' Aunt Clara sighs. 'They haven't got their fourth member, have they?'

'No, but it won't be long before they do.'

'We need your help,' Holly says, putting her knife and fork down. 'We don't know what to do.'

'Funnily enough, they had the cheek to come into the shop earlier,' Aunt Clara says.

I stare at her. 'What? Why?'

'They wanted to put a poster in the window for some kind of fundraiser they're doing. It was very strange. I mean, after what happened the last time they were here. You'd think they'd know to stay away.'

I glance around the kitchen and shudder, remembering how the Blood Witches had almost burnt it to the ground. 'What did you say to them?'

'I told them to get out. That they were barred for good. It was very awkward though. I'd never normally turn down a charity request.'

'I think you did the right thing,' I say. 'The fundraiser's for Eve's brother – to help pay for him to go to America.'

Aunt Clara looks confused. 'But surely that's a good thing.'

'It's a good thing but for very bad reasons,' Holly says.

Aunt Clara frowns. 'What do you mean?'

'We think they're only doing it to make Eve so grateful that she joins them,' I explain.

Aunt Clara looks horrified. 'But that – that's awful.' I feel dread ripple across the table from her.

'It's so frustrating,' I say. 'I thought it would have been easier for us to get people to join us because they're so horrible. But they're so good at tricking people and appearing nice.'

'What should we do?' Holly asks. 'How can we stop them?'

We all sit in silence for a moment.

'You need to find their weaknesses and use them to your advantage,' Aunt Clara replies.

'Are you sure they have any weaknesses?' I find it hard to imagine Izzy having any kind of weakness.

'Oh, everyone has a weakness,' Aunt Clara replies.

The phone starts to ring. Aunt Clara stands up. 'I'm so sorry, I'm going to have to take that. I'm expecting a call from a local author about doing a book-signing in the shop.'

As Clara leaves the room Holly and I look at each other.

'What are their weaknesses?' Holly asks.

'Stephen?' I say. 'His lack of brainpower definitely makes him the weakest link.'

'Ha! Yeah. What else?'

An idea starts forming in my mind. 'What about their greed?'

'How do you mean?'

'Well, they're so desperate for power, right? They'll stop at nothing.'

'But isn't that what makes them so strong? The fact that they'll stop at nothing?'

'Maybe. Or maybe not. Think about it. What happened when we were desperate to talk to Eve?'

Holly sighs. 'We really messed up.'

'Exactly. We wanted to get to her so badly we totally messed up.'

'But the Blood Witches aren't like that. They're so calculating.'

'Yes, but only because they haven't really been tested.'

'How do you mean?'

'Well, I hate to say it but we have kind of made things easy for them. We messed things up with Eve, which meant she didn't want anything to do with us. Which made it all the easier for them to sneak in and make friends.'

Holly frowns. 'So, what are you saying we have to do?'

'We have to get smarter. We have to make them panic so that they mess up.' I smile at Holly defiantly. 'We have to play them at their own game.'

14

The next day, Holly and I decide to go to The Cup and Saucer for a post-Science-homework treat. I've brought Ellie along too. Not literally, obviously, as she's in London, but on FaceTime. I put my phone on the table, propped up against a bowl of sugar sachets.

'Is he there?' mini-Ellie whispers from the screen.

'Is who here?' I say, knowing exactly who she means. Unlike Holly, Ellie doesn't have an irrational dislike of Niall. It's been great that one of my best friends likes him and that I've had someone to talk about him with but I don't think here is the best place.

'Mr Seriously-Cute-With-a-Capital-C,' Ellie says. 'Is he working today?'

I ignore Holly's laboured sigh and glance around the café. There's no sign of Niall and my heart sinks. 'I don't think so,' I say. 'Oh, hang on.' The door to the kitchen opens and Niall comes striding out holding a handful of flyers.

'What?' Ellie squeals. 'Is he there?'

Niall starts heading over in our direction, putting flyers on each of the tables.

'Shh!' I hiss at the phone. 'Don't say anything!'

Niall puts a flyer down on the table next to ours, looking at me the whole time.

Ellie's eyes widen. 'Is he there?' she whispers.

'Shhh!' I shake my head at the phone.

Across from me, Holly starts to smirk.

'Hey,' Niall says, coming over to stand by Holly, still looking straight at me. 'Is everything OK?'

'Yes of course. Why shouldn't it be?' I reply.

Niall grins, and his eyes start twinkling and his cheeks start dimpling . . . and my heart starts pounding. 'It looked as if you were talking to the sugar bowl.'

Holly coughs down a laugh. Ellie mouths '*OMG!*' From where Niall is standing he can't see the phone.

'No,' I say, as breezily as I can. 'I was talking to Holly and looking at the sugar bowl.' Because that's normal. Nice one, Nessa!

Niall half smiles, half frowns. 'Oh . . . OK.'

'It's a really nice bowl,' I say lamely. Out of the corner of my eye I see Ellie on my phone, flailing about like she's dying.

'Do you think?' Niall stares down at the plain white bowl. 'I prefer the salt and pepper pots, personally.'

Holly gives a long drawn-out sigh. 'Wow, this has got to be the most boring conversation ever! I'm just going to go to the toilet. I'll have a chocolate milkshake,' she says to Niall as she gets up to leave. 'Whenever you're ready to take our order.'

I squirm at how rude she sounds but Niall seems

completely unfazed. 'Sure,' he says with a nod.

We both watch as Holly makes her way to the back of the café. Then I look back at my phone. Ellie's bouncing around with glee. I grab the phone and hear a tiny '*Nooooo!*' before ending the call. Thankfully, Niall doesn't seem to notice.

'I'm really sorry about the other day,' he says, running his hand through his hair.

'What other day?' I say jauntily, like getting rejected at an audition is such a trivial thing to me I forget it the second it's over.

'The audition. I'm sorry you weren't old enough.'

Hearing those words stings all over again. I take a deep breath and force myself to smile. 'Oh, it's fine. I understand.'

Niall leans on the back of Holly's chair. His arms look so strong. I picture one of them round my shoulders and feel all tingly inside. 'We all loved the way you played.'

'Seriously, you don't have to say that. It's OK.'

'I know I don't *have* to say it,' Niall says,

looking me straight in the eyes. 'I want to.'

'Oh.' *Say something else!* I yell at myself inside my head. *Say something more!* But the only word I can find is boring old *oh*.

'I really loved playing with you that time on New Year's Eve too.' Niall smiles at me again but this time it isn't one of his cheeky grins, it's softer, more meaningful. I feel my heart start to melt.

'You did?' I think back to that night, the two of us standing right next to each other, Niall's bow arm moving so fast over his fiddle that it practically blurred, my fingers gliding over the guitar strings, playing in perfect harmony. It was as if the music was connecting us like an invisible cord. For a moment I feel that connection between us again, like if he were to move, I'd have to move in sync. But then, in an instant, it's gone.

Niall puts a flyer down on the table. I feel a bitter pang as I see that it's for the fund-raising fete. Then a terrible thought occurs to me – does Niall know

Izzy and the others? Is that why he's handing out the leaflet? Is he their friend?

'What's this for?' I ask casually, picking up the flyer.

Niall shrugs. 'I don't know. My boss just asked me to put some out on the tables.'

I quickly skim the words on the flyer. 'Oh, it's for a fete,' I say, as if I don't already know and I haven't been thinking of nothing else for the last twenty-four hours. 'Looks like it's for a great cause.'

Niall doesn't say anything; he just takes his notepad from the back pocket of his jeans. The air between us feels empty.

'Should be fun,' I try again.

Niall looks around the café. 'I guess.'

My head fills with an Instagram-style feed of images of Niall and me at the fete. Checking out the stalls together. Niall winning me a teddy bear on the coconut shy. Eating candyfloss by the carousel. 'Do you – do you think you'll be going?'

He shakes his head. 'Nah. It's not really my kind

of thing.' He takes a pencil from behind his ear and gets ready to write my order. 'So, what can I get you?'

I look at him for a moment, aware that something has changed but not sure what or why. And then I have a horrible thought. Does talking about fetes being fun make me seem really young?

'We'll have two chocolate milkshakes, please,' I mutter, actually feeling relieved to see Holly on her way back from the toilet.

'Sure.' Niall puts his pad back in his pocket and walks over to the counter, without giving me a second glance.

'Everything OK?' Holly asks as she sits down.

I nod, even though my throat feels choked with disappointment. There's no point talking to Holly about it though, not with the way she feels about Niall. So I shove down my disappointment and hand her the flyer instead. 'Look.'

'Wow, they really are going all out, aren't they?' She squeezes my hand. 'Don't worry. Remember what we talked about last night. They're not going to win.'

I nod but I feel a hollow ache inside. The fact is, raising money to help George *is* a good thing. If we do anything that jeopardises that we'll be hurting him and Eve's family. Arrghh! Why is everything so complicated?

I'd hoped that I'd feel a bit better after our milkshakes but, if anything, seeing Niall flitting about the café without once looking at me made me feel even worse. As soon as I get back to Paper Soul I head straight to my bedroom without even saying hello to Aunt Clara and fling myself on my bed. The alert goes off on my phone. A text from Ellie.

I can't believe you cut me off like that! What happened? Did he ask you out? Did you ever stop talking about the sugar bowl? I need answers!! Xx

I put the phone down on my bedside cabinet.

I can't bring myself to tell Ellie what happened yet. It'll be too rubbish having to relive it. I pick up my guitar and start to play but my fingers feel clunky and awkward and all of the chords sound out of tune.

'Nessa, are you OK?' Aunt Clara calls up the stairs.

'Yes, I'm fine,' I call back. Part of me wants to run downstairs and ask for a hug. But then she'd want to know what was wrong and then I'd have to tell her about Niall. And knowing my luck she'd probably tell me that she thinks I'm too young for him too. Or, even worse, she'd tell me that I shouldn't be thinking about boys anyway because I need all of my energy to fight the Blood Witches. Instinctively I feel for my mum's locket in my pocket. I wrap my hands around it and lie down on my bed, staring out of the window. The evening sky is turning an inky blue and I can just make out the first pale stars beginning to shine.

'How did you deal with it?' I whisper to the sky,

as if my mum's sitting up there on one of the stars. 'How did you cope with the pressure?'

I close my eyes and although I don't hear anything, a picture enters my mind. At first I think it's the memory of an old photograph – the photo Dad has of him and Mum sitting on a see-saw in the park. But then the figures in the photo start to move. Dad pushes down hard on the see-saw, causing Mum to bounce into the air, her long blonde hair cascading out around her. As she shrieks with laughter, Dad gets off the see-saw and walks over to her. She stands up and he pulls her into a hug. I feel a surge of joy spreading through my body and my skin starts to tingle.

'I love you, Celeste,' I hear my dad whisper. And then the picture fades.

I lie on my bed, my skin still tingling. What just happened? Did I get a flashback about my mum because I'm holding her locket? Then I realise that it doesn't really matter *how* I got the vision. What matters is that my mum was happy despite being a Silver Witch. She was still able to meet someone and fall in love. And if she did, then so can I. The only reason it all went so wrong for my mum was because of the Blood Witches, blackmailing her to join them to save my life, the way Izzy and the others are about to do with Eve. I feel a sudden surge of determination and I put the locket back in my pocket and sit up. The Blood Witches might have been able to get my mum to join them but they won't get Eve. I'm going to make sure of it.

15

'Listen up, everybody, I've got some great news,' Mr Bailey says, beaming down at us from the stage.

A hush descends on the school hall. I look at Holly and pull a face. The last time Mr Bailey used that line in an assembly it was to tell us that the school had started a homework club – which is only ever 'great news' on the planet Head Teacher.

'Actually, I think it would be really nice if the students concerned could share the news with you themselves.' Mr Bailey looks out into the sea of students. 'Izzy, Vivien, Stephen – would you like to come up on to the stage?'

'Oh no,' Holly mutters.

I watch as Izzy leaps to her feet, her glossy lips pulled into a smug smile. She smooths down her hair and starts sashaying her way to the front of the hall, with Vivien and Stephen close behind. Mr Bailey beams at them as they go up on to the stage. If only he knew the truth. If only he knew what they were capable of.

'Izzy, would you like to share the news with your fellow students?' he asks.

Izzy smiles at Mr Bailey. 'Of course, sir.' She turns to face us. 'We're going to be holding a fete here on Saturday and we'd love you all to be involved.' Her smile fades and her eyes widen. 'The reason it's at such short notice is because it's for a very important and urgent cause.' I look around at the other students. They're all gazing up at her as if they're hypnotised. All apart from Eve, who's staring at her feet, cheeks flushed. 'I'm sure you all know our good friend Eve Hart,' Izzy continues. A few of the students in our class look at each other and raise their eyebrows. Good friend? They haven't forgotten how Izzy and the others used to make Eve's life hell. 'Well, her brother was in a terrible accident a while ago and it's left him unable to walk.' Izzy voice actually cracks at this point, as if she might be about to cry. I make a mental note to tell her that if the witch thing doesn't work out she should definitely become an actress. 'We're holding the fete to raise money to send him to America for surgery. That might be his only hope,' Izzy says melodramatically and Eve flinches.

'Wow,' Holly mutters. 'If she doesn't stop soon I think I'm going to be sick.'

I nod, watching as Izzy looks back at Mr Bailey.

'Well, I don't know about you, but I think that deserves a massive round of applause,' he says, clapping his hands together like a performing seal. Applause ripples out around the hall. The louder it gets, the more smug the smiles on Izzy, Vivien and Stephen's faces become. I look at Eve. She isn't clapping. Her hands are thrust deep into her blazer pockets and she's looking as if she wants the ground to open up and swallow her whole. I feel a pinprick of hope.

'These students are setting such a wonderful example for Fairhollow High – and our motto, Service Before Self,' Mr Bailey continues.

'Seriously?' Holly says, pretending to retch.

'And to support them in their endeavour,' Mr Bailey continues, 'first period lessons are cancelled today and you're to go to your form rooms instead to plan for the fete.'

A murmur of appreciation spreads around the hall.

'Izzy, Vivien and Stephen will be visiting each form and allocating you a stall.' Mr Bailey strides to the front of the stage and stares at us all enthusiastically. 'Let's all get behind this fantastic initiative and help Eve's brother on his road to recovery.'

Izzy, Vivien and Stephen leave the stage to another burst of applause. Eve digs her hands deeper into her pockets.

Back in our form room, Mr Matthews is bouncing around with excitement like a proud grandfather. 'This is wonderful, absolutely wonderful!' he says, clasping his bony hands together. 'You're a credit to this class, Izzy, Vivien and Stephen.'

Izzy shakes her head. 'Seriously, sir, it's the least we could do – for our friend.' She puts her arm round Eve's shoulder. Eve smiles. I cringe.

'So, what stall would you like us to run?' Mr Matthews asks, perching down on the edge of his desk.

'I thought maybe we could do the cake stall,' Izzy says.

Holly lets out a snort of laughter. 'Are you serious?'

Izzy scowls at her. 'Why, what's wrong with that?'

'After what happened the last time you guys did some baking?' Holly says, her eyes sparking with anger.

I feel her rage mix with my own as I remember

153

that day in Paper Soul when the Blood Witches purposefully burnt some of Aunt Clara's cakes and the oven caught fire. I stare hard at Izzy. *You won't get away with this*, I think, imagining boring the words into her head. The colour drains from her face and she looks away.

'Well – uh – it doesn't have to be the cake stall,' she mutters. Vivien and Stephen look at her in shock. I feel a glimmer of excitement. It worked! I was able to transfer my thought into her mind. I sit back in my chair, feeling drained from the effort but elated at this latest development.

'Er, yes it does,' Vivien snaps, glaring at Holly. 'We've got it all planned out.'

'Oh, I bet you have,' Holly mutters.

'Really, Holly,' Mr Matthews says, peering at her over his half-moon glasses. 'Your classmates are trying to organise a fete for a very worthwhile cause. I think you could be a little more supportive.'

'Yeah, Holly,' Stephen says with a sly grin.

Holly glares at him and pointedly taps her finger

on her eyebrow. He looks away, his face flushing an angry red, clearly still scarred from the Bunsen burner 'accident'.

'So, that's settled, then,' Mr Matthews says, getting off his desk and walking around to his chair. 'Our form will be doing the cake stall. Izzy, Vivien, Stephen – would you like to get off to the other classes and we'll get on with some planning?'

'Yes, sir. Thank you, sir,' Izzy says.

'Three bags full, sir,' Holly mutters.

At lunchtime the canteen is buzzing with talk of the fete.

'I know they're doing this for all the wrong reasons,' I say to Holly as I take my lunch from my bag, 'but at least they'll raise some money for Eve's brother. At least something good will come of it.'

'Hmm.' Holly bites down hard on her sausage roll, causing flakes of pastry to cascade down her chin.

'OK, let's decide what cakes we're going to

make.' I search in my bag for a pen but my pencil case is missing. I get up. 'I left my pencil case in English. Back in a sec.'

Holly nods and takes another mouthful of sausage roll.

When I get to the English classroom I hear the rumble of conversation from inside and a burst of laughter. I push the door open and see Izzy, Vivien and Stephen sat on one of the tables. They're looking very pleased with themselves.

'I think it could be thousands,' Izzy says, studying a sheet of paper in her hand.

As soon as I walk in and they see me, hatred hits me like a sharp gust of icy wind. I head over to the table I'd been sitting at and grab my pencil case.

'Well, look who it is,' Vivien says.

'How does it feel to be such a loser?' Stephen says, getting down from the table and glaring at me.

'How am I a loser?' I say to him, trying to ignore the nausea bubbling in my stomach, caused by their hatred.

Stephen laughs. 'How are you a loser?' He turns to Izzy.

Izzy simply smiles sweetly. 'Ah, don't be mean, Stephen. You know it's not nice to pick on those less fortunate than yourself.'

'Oh yes, and you guys are all about helping the less fortunate, aren't you?' I snap.

Izzy widens her eyes as if I've really hurt her. 'What are you trying to say, Nessa? Were you just making fun of Eve's brother? Wow, that's harsh.'

I feel my thoughts tangling up in knots. She knows I wasn't trying to say that but I bet this is how she'll twist it when she reports back to Eve. Crap! This is not how I'd wanted things to go. I take a deep breath and remember my conversation with Holly last night. We need to target their weak spot. 'I was actually talking about Stephen.'

Stephen frowns and gets down off the desk. 'What do you mean?'

I smile at him knowingly. 'Oh, I'm sure you'll figure it out. Eventually.' I focus all of my attention on him and picture the words *IZZY AND VIVIEN ARE USING YOU* in huge letters, projecting into his mind. At first, nothing seems to happen. Then Stephen scratches his head and his face flushes.

'I don't know – I don't know what you're talking about,' he mumbles. But he's not looking at me any more. He's looking at Izzy and Vivien and he's frowning.

I feel light-headed from a mixture of the effort of projecting my thoughts and excitement that it seems to have worked again.

I look at Izzy and treat her to one of her own sickly-sweet-style smiles. 'Yes, we'll see who the real losers are,' I say, before picking up my pencil case, turning and heading to the door.

The silence in the classroom behind me is deafening.

16

'This is so frustrating!' Holly exclaims as we watch Vivien and Stephen hoisting a huge banner advertising the fete over the school entrance, while Izzy shouts instructions. 'Everywhere we look there's stuff about the fete. It's like they're rubbing our noses in it. It's like they're taking out adverts telling us that they've won.'

'They haven't won,' I say firmly, taking Holly's arm and steering her away.

It's lunchtime the next day and the school looks like the set for one of those home makeover shows, with posters, banners and bunting advertising the fete being draped over every available wall space.

'We should tell Mr Bailey,' Holly says, her eyes

wide with indignation. 'We should tell him what they're up to.'

'Oh yeah, great plan,' I say sarcastically. 'And what would we say? *Oh, hi, Mr Bailey. You know how you think that Izzy, Vivien and Stephen are the most caring human beings since Mother Theresa? Well, actually they're witches and they're only putting on this fete so that they can complete their pente first and use their evil powers to ruin everyone's lives.* Yeah, I can see him being fine with that.'

We look at each other for a moment, then sigh.

'Come on, let's go to the girls' toilets,' Holly says, heading towards the door. 'It's about the only place that hasn't been fete-ed.'

As soon as we enter the toilets, Holly frowns and nods towards the cubicle doors. One of them is closed. I'm about to make some small talk with Holly about the weather when I hear a sob coming from the cubicle.

'But I don't understand,' a voice gasps. 'I thought there was a chance.'

Holly and I look at each other, rooted to the spot.

'But that's not what they said before,' the voice says, louder and clearer this time.

'Eve?' I mouth to Holly. She nods.

'But the doctor in London said he might walk again one day,' Eve splutters between sobs. 'He said there was hope. What's changed?'

I feel a deep, deep sorrow seeping out from under the cubicle door, engulfing me like a thick fog. I beckon at Holly to follow me and we tiptoe out of the toilets. There's no way we should be eavesdropping on such a personal conversation.

'Wow, that sounded intense,' Holly says as soon as we're in the corridor.

I nod. 'It must be bad news about her brother.' I shake my arms, trying to get rid of the sorrow still clinging to me. 'I wish we could comfort her. I wish she didn't think we were . . .'

'Crazy people? Freaks?' Holly says.

I nod.

Holly sighs. 'And she thinks the sun shines out

of Izzy's backside. Oh, the irony. Come on, the bell will be going soon. Let's get to History.'

I follow her up the corridor, my heart heavy.

There's no sign of Eve in History. She must have gone home. I'm glad. She's way better off being with her family than getting false sympathy from Izzy, Vivien and Stephen. Miss Maxwell sets us a multiple-choice test and although I don't normally enjoy tests, for once I'm relieved. I need something else to focus on, something to give my brain a rest from thinking about the Blood Witches. But I'm only two questions in when I hear Izzy and Vivien whispering at the table behind me.

'Turns out I'm a great doctor,' Vivien says and Izzy laughs.

Then Vivien whispers something else. I can't make out what it is exactly but I do hear the words 'never walk again' and 'have to go to America'.

The hairs on the back of my neck prickle.

'She totally believed it?' I hear Izzy say.

'Yep. Fell for it hook, line and sinker,' Vivien replies.

I stare down at my test. All of the questions blur into a huge jumbled mass of letters. The only questions I can think about now are to do with the Blood Witches. Was it Vivien on the phone to Eve in the toilets, using her mimic powers to pretend to be a doctor? But why would a doctor call Eve? That doesn't make sense. I lean back slightly in my chair, straining to hear what Vivien is saying.

'I guess her mum must be as gullible as she is,' Vivien mutters.

'Yeah, like mother like daughter,' Izzy whispers.

'The best thing is, now they think their only hope is going to America, they're going to be even more grateful to us for helping them raise money.'

Miss Maxwell looks up and frowns at Vivien. 'Shhh,' she says.

'Sorry, miss,' Vivien calls back.

I glance at Holly. She's staring down at the table,

looking as horrified as I feel. She must have heard them too.

The rest of the lesson drags by so slowly that at one point, I'm sure the class clock is going backwards. But finally the bell for the end of school rings. Holly and I race out. We don't say a word to each other until we're halfway down the driveway.

'What are they playing at?' I ask Holly.

'You heard what Vivien said. To make Eve even more grateful to them for organising the fete,' Holly says.

'But surely she'd be grateful enough as it was? Why would they want to hurt her even more?'

'Because they're evil.' Holly sighs in frustration.

'This is so horrible,' I say, shivering even though the sun is shining. 'Think of what Eve's family must be going through right now.' I grab hold of Holly's arm. 'We need to tell them. We need to tell them that it isn't true.'

Holly shakes her head. 'How can we? Eve and her mum already hate us and think we're out to cause them pain. If we turn up now and tell them the phone call was someone playing a trick on them they'll never believe us. Or they might even think that we're behind it. And Eve will hate us even more.'

I look down at the ground in despair.

Holly links her arm in mine. 'Come on.'

'Where are we going?'

'To the place that always makes you feel better,' she replies. 'The oak tree.'

17

The night before the fete I barely sleep a wink and whenever I do drift off I'm plunged straight into a nightmare about the Blood Witches – Izzy and Vivien cackling as they take all of the money from the Paper Soul tills, Stephen ghosting through the walls of Aunt Clara's house, putting up banners saying *BLOOD WITCHES RULE!* As soon as the dawn light starts creeping its way through the crack between my curtains I get up. I want to lose myself in playing my guitar but I don't want to wake Aunt Clara so I text my dad instead. It's late morning where he is and I'm hoping to catch him on a break.

Hey, are you free for a chat? Lol xxx

I sit cross-legged on my bed, staring down at the phone, willing it to ring. Talking to Dad will remind me that there is a life outside of Fairhollow, away from the Blood Witches. But the phone stays silent. I go over to the window and stare outside. The brown-tiled rooftops and lopsided chimney stacks look so quaint and olde worlde and the sunlight is making everything shimmer gold. It all looks so perfect, so normal. I think of the fete, of Izzy and Stephen and Vivien being treated like superheroes. What if they make their move today? What if they approach Eve about becoming a Blood Witch and she's so grateful she joins them? I'll have no way of stopping them, especially with Holly away for the weekend with her parents again. Once a witch chooses a side, that's it. If they change their minds, as my mum tragically found out, it leads to fatal consequences.

Fear begins twisting my stomach into knots.

I hear Aunt Clara moving about and I feel a burst of relief. I need to tell her how I'm feeling. I need to ask her advice. I put on my dressing gown and head downstairs.

When I get to the kitchen Aunt Clara's standing by the stove, heating some almond milk in a pan. She's wearing her long emerald-green dressing gown, which always makes her hair look even redder.

'You're up very early for a Saturday,' she says, looking at me concerned. 'Are you OK?'

'Yes, yes, I'm fine.' I sit down at the table and try to look calm. I don't want to panic her.

'Er, Nessa, aren't you forgetting something?' She takes a pack of porridge oats from the cupboard then turns to face me.

'What?'

She smiles. 'You can't fool an empath. My powers might be fading but I'm definitely sensing a lot of worry coming off you.'

I can't help laughing and throw my hands up in mock surrender. 'OK. OK. I'm just really worried about the fete. What if Eve joins the Blood Witches? What are we going to do?'

Aunt Clara takes the pan from the stove and comes and sits down beside me. 'Do you really think that's going to happen today?'

I start picking at a crack in the wooden table. 'Why not? I mean, after they've given Eve the money for her brother she's going to be so grateful.'

Aunt Clara frowns. 'Yes, but look at how she reacted when you and Holly tried to get her to join you. You said yourself that she might not be able to control her powers and she might feel guilty over what she did.'

'I know, but we hadn't done anything nice for her beforehand. We just barged into her home without any thought. The Blood Witches have taken their time; they've earned her trust – even though they really don't deserve it.'

Aunt Clara nods thoughtfully. 'How about I come with you today? Make sure nothing bad happens.'

I stare at her. 'Really? But what about the shop?'

'I'm sure Dawn can manage on her own for a while.' Aunt Clara takes hold of my hand. 'You shouldn't have to deal with this on your own. It's too much.'

I feel a surge of love coming from her into me. It's warm and comforting and evaporates my fear. 'Thank you.'

'You're very welcome.' Aunt Clara stands up and walks back over to the stove. 'Now, let's have some breakfast. Things always seem better after a bowl of almond-milk porridge.'

There was a time when I would have seriously doubted that statement, but not any more. Right now I can't think of anything more comforting.

Aunt Clara and I spend the morning making brownies for the cake stall and get to the school mid-afternoon when the fete's in full swing. The school field is full of stalls trimmed with brightly coloured bunting, and jaunty music is crackling over the tannoy. The place is packed with students and their families. It's horrible to think that something so bright and cheery could be so dark at heart. It's like a stick of pink rock with the word *EVIL* running through it.

'Let's get these brownies to the cake stall,' Aunt Clara says, squeezing my arm.

As we walk past the tombola I see Vivien talking to the student running the stall.

'We've taken almost three hundred pounds,' the girl says to Vivien excitedly.

Vivien smiles triumphantly. 'Good work. But I'm sure you can make even more. Think of poor Eve's brother.'

'Of course,' the girl replies before calling out to people to have a go.

My stomach churns and I turn away.

'Don't let it get to you,' Aunt Clara says, striding ahead.

'But how?' I ask, running to keep up. 'What they're doing is so wrong.'

Aunt Clara stops and looks at me. Her eyes are ringed with even more black liner than usual. I wonder if she did it on purpose, to make herself look fiercer. If so, it's definitely worked. 'Remember what I said to you and Holly about the Blood Witches being their own worst enemies?'

I nod.

'Well, this is a perfect example. They weren't content with putting on the fete to try to win Eve's support – their greed has made them use it as a way to steal money too. That's how they'll come unstuck, you wait and see.'

I nod, wishing I could believe her.

When we get to the cake stall Mr Matthews throws up his hands joyfully. 'Clara, my dear!' he exclaims, dropping his pen on to a plate of jam tarts in excitement. 'How lovely to see you.' He turns to me and grins. 'It's been an absolute delight, teaching another Hamilton girl. And isn't she so like Celeste?'

Aunt Clara nods and they both look at me wistfully, as if they're thinking of my mum. I feel a double pang of sorrow mingling with my own. I seem to be picking up on things way too easily today. The stress of the fete must be making me super-sensitive. I shove the feelings down. I can't afford to get upset today. I have to stay strong.

'How's it going, Mr Matthews?' Izzy comes breezing over, grinning like she just won the lottery. She's wearing a T-shirt with the word *LOVE* emblazoned across it. The O in *LOVE* is a heart made from sequins. I fight the urge to ask her if the store ran out of tops with the word *HATE* on. 'Oh, hi, Nessa,' Izzy says sweetly. Then she looks at the cake tin Aunt Clara's carrying. 'Are those for the stall?'

Aunt Clara nods, her lips pursed together.

'So kind of you. I'm such a great fan of your baking.'

I hear Aunt Clara give a short, sharp gasp and I feel anger rolling off her in hot waves, making my face burn.

Izzy takes the tin and passes it to Mr Matthews.

'How much money have you raised so far, sir?'

Mr Matthews scratches his head. 'Oh dear, I'm afraid I don't know. We've been so busy I haven't had the chance to count it yet.'

Izzy pats him on the arm. 'Don't worry, sir. I'll count it for you.'

'Would you?' Mr Matthews hands her the cash tin. 'That's very kind of you.'

I feel more red-hot anger coming from Aunt Clara and I start feeling faint.

'No problem at all.' Izzy opens the cash box. It's full of notes, which she stuffs into her jeans pocket, a sly smile dancing on her lips. It takes every muscle in my body to stop me from leaping over and grabbing it from her.

'OK, well, I'd love to stay and chat but I've got a fete to run,' Izzy says, coming out from behind the stall. 'And money to count,' she says quietly as she walks past me.

My head starts to pound. Behind me there's a loud crack as someone knocks a coconut from the shy. It's so loud it feels as if it's split my brain in two.

'It's lovely what they're doing,' Mr Matthews says, gazing after Izzy proudly. His words echo round my mind. '*Lovely-lovely-lovely . . . doing-doing-doing.*'

I turn away feeling sick.

The next hour passes by in a haze. My headache gets worse and worse. Everywhere I look is like viewing a badly tuned TV. The colours are too bright, the music, chatter and laughter too loud. Even though I'm careful to avoid getting too close to Izzy, Stephen and Vivien I can feel their evil hanging over the field like a thick, polluted smog. Finally, the fete comes to a close and Mr Bailey asks us all to gather around a small stage in the centre of the field. Eve and her mum and dad are standing awkwardly beside him. They all look pale and drawn with dark circles ringing their eyes. They must be so devastated about George. *It isn't even true*, I want to rush over and tell them. *There is still hope.*

Izzy, Vivien and Stephen walk over. Izzy's holding a cash box. I wish I could tell everyone

175

their real motives. But then *I'd* look like the nasty one, trying to cause trouble at a charity fete. I fold my arms tightly, trying to make myself feel stronger and more solid.

'Let's have a big round of applause for the students who've worked so tirelessly to make this day happen and at such short notice,' Mr Bailey booms into the microphone. 'Izzy, Vivien and Stephen.'

Everyone starts clapping and cheering. Eve's parents look at Izzy so gratefully and it makes me feel so sick I have to lean on Aunt Clara for support.

'Are you OK?' she whispers.

I nod. But I feel horrible. Like I'm trapped in a nightmare I can't wake up from.

'Thank you. Thank you so much,' Izzy says breathlessly into the microphone, beaming her fake smile around the crowd. 'But really it's Eve's family who deserve the applause.' She switches her expression to sorrowful. 'They've been through so much.'

Everyone starts clapping again and Eve's mum wipes a tear from her eye.

'We've just added up all of the takings from today,' Izzy says, waving the cash box in front of her. 'And I'm so happy to tell you that we've raised almost one thousand pounds.' She looks at Eve's parents. 'I know it isn't enough to get George to America but this is just the start. Vivien, Stephen and I are going to keep on arranging charity events until we do.' She hands the cash box to Eve's mum.

Eve's mum hugs her and my stomach churns.

'And now there's just one more thing left to do,' Izzy says, picking up a bucket from the floor. 'We need to announce the winner of the raffle! Mr Bailey, would you like to choose the winning ticket?'

I see Vivien and Stephen exchanging sly smirks as Mr Bailey bounds over. 'Of course!' He puts his hand in the bucket and pulls out a ticket. 'And the winner is . . .' he says, unfolding the ticket, 'number two hundred and thirty-three.'

'That's me,' a boy cries from behind me.

I turn and see Vivien's brother, holding a ticket in the air. My skin prickles with suspicion. Have the Blood Witches somehow rigged the raffle so they win that too?

'Congratulations!' Mr Bailey says. 'You've won a guitar, very kindly donated by the music store on the High Street.'

As Vivien's brother goes up to collect his prize I glance at Izzy. She's looking straight at me with a knowing smile. *We've won and there's nothing you can do about it*, it seems to say. I turn away.

'Ooh, one last thing,' Izzy says into the microphone. 'We're having an after-party at my house to celebrate the success of the fete and you're all welcome.'

I glance at Aunt Clara. She's looking as unimpressed as I feel. The thought of going to Izzy's house is horrible. It's been bad enough being in the same field as them all afternoon. But if I don't go, I won't be able to keep an eye on them and Eve.

Aunt Clara touches my arm. 'Do you want me to go instead?' she says.

'How did you . . .? Oh!' I smile, realising she must have picked up on my thoughts. 'Are you sure?'

Aunt Clara nods. 'Izzy's mother and I go way back. It might be good to let her know that I'm practising again; that you and Holly aren't the only Silver Witches in Fairhollow.'

I hug her. 'Thank you.'

'You go straight home and rest,' Aunt Clara says. 'You look washed out.'

I frown. 'But will you be OK, going there on your own?'

Aunt Clara nods, her red bob swishing. 'Of course. I'll go with Mr Matthews. We can reminisce about how I used to make his life hell. I'll be fine.'

Feeling reassured, I turn and head off home. But when I get to the turning to the High Street I can't resist following the path up to the tree instead. After all the stress of this afternoon I'm hoping it will make me feel strong again. I sit down, in between its huge, gnarly roots and lean back against the trunk. But instead of feeling its strength tingling into my back, all of the tension and anger and hurt of today comes bubbling up through my body and I start to cry. I picture Eve at Izzy's party, overcome with gratitude and agreeing to join the Blood Witches. Then I think of my mum going from Silver to Blood Witch to save my life. As I sit there sobbing all of the deepest, darkest thoughts I've been keeping bottled up finally come out. It's because of my mum's terrible choice that I'm still alive. She chose to join them so that I'd be cured from a terrible childhood illness. And then she died in a spell that went wrong. It's because of that terrible choice, that she's dead. I'm to blame for my mum's death. I feel overcome with grief. And now I've started it feels as if I'll never be able to stop crying.

But slowly, as the sun dips down behind the trees, the pain begins to fade. Eventually I get to my feet, clutching Mum's locket in my hand. What happened to her is a tragedy but there's nothing I can do about it now. It's done. The Blood Witches haven't won yet. Even if they do get Eve to join them, they'll still only have four. There will still be hope. And while there's still hope, I can't give up.

I walk back down the path, repeating those words over and over in my head. *I can't give up. I can't give up.*

18

When I get back to Paper Soul I help Dawn clean the café and shut up the shop. Then I head straight to the kitchen and make myself a hot chocolate. I wonder how Aunt Clara's getting on at the party. My phone pings with a text from Holly.

How did it go? Hxx

Not great. How's it going with your parents? Xoxo

They've taken me to the theatre to see a play about a court case!!! Can you believe it? Even when they're not at work they're going to plays

about work!!! ☹ **What do you mean not great?**
They haven't got Eve to join them have they?! Hxx

No – at least I don't think so. Really missed you
today xoxo

Really miss you too! Hxx

I put my phone on the table and take a sip of
hot chocolate. A combination of the sweet warmth
of the drink and Holly's texts makes me feel slightly
better. I imagine a best-case scenario. The Blood
Witches' plan doesn't work. Eve doesn't join them.
Her brother starts walking again. We tell her the
truth and she joins us instead. It feels about as
believable as a fairy tale.

I hear the door downstairs slam shut and
footsteps on the stairs. Aunt Clara! Please let there
be good news. I get to my feet as she walks into the
kitchen and search her face for clues. Her face is
creased into a frown, with two grooves etched into

the space between her eyebrows like a claw-print. This is not good.

'How did it go?' I say, barely daring to ask.

Aunt Clara sits down heavily on the chair beside me and kicks off her shoes. 'Not good,' she says glumly. 'Not good at all.'

I sit back down. 'Why? What happened?' Dread grips my head like a vice. 'Eve didn't join them, did she?'

'No. Not yet, anyhow.'

'What do you mean, not yet?'

'I'd forgotten exactly what we're up against.' Aunt Clara starts rubbing her temples. I've never seen her looking so stressed. Not even when Izzy nearly burnt down her kitchen. 'That girl's parents are pure evil.'

I imagine Clara at my age and how similar our lives must have been, with her and my mum battling Izzy's mum and dad. And then a horrible thought occurs to me. 'Were Izzy's parents involved in getting my mum to become a Blood Witch?'

Aunt Clara nods. Now she looks close to tears. 'I thought I could block it all out by not practising any more. I thought I could pretend it never happened. Even when you came here and I realised that it would be impossible to ignore . . . I didn't realise how painful it would be, seeing them again. And seeing that nothing has changed.'

'What do you mean?'

'Izzy's parents are in on this plan of theirs. Today, at the party, her dad kept following Eve's parents around, spying on them.'

'How?'

'His power is invisibility. I could sense him there, hovering around them all the time, obviously trying to hear things that Izzy and the others could use to their advantage.' Aunt Clara leans back in her chair and looks at me. 'I don't know how we're going to beat them, Nessa.'

That night I can't sleep. I lie on my bed beneath the window with the curtains open wide and gaze up at the stars. *What shall I do?* I ask, over and over again. *How can we beat them?* But every idea that comes to me is more ludicrous than the last. When I start to seriously consider kidnapping Eve to keep her out of the Blood Witches' clutches I know I need to give up. I roll on to my side and close my eyes. Hopefully when Holly's back we can come up with something. On Monday in school we'll have a breakthrough, I tell myself, before finally falling into a fitful sleep.

The Blood Witches make their next move before registration has even begun.

'Eve, Eve, we got you a present!' Izzy exclaims as she, Stephen and Vivien walk through the door.

Eve looks up from her desk and starts to smile. 'Really? What is it?'

Izzy puts a carrier bag down on the table in front of her. 'Open it and see.'

Holly and I watch as Eve slides a box from the bag. 'An iPad?' she gasps, her cheeks flushing.

'Yep.' Izzy glances at me triumphantly.

Eve frowns. 'But I don't understand. They're so expensive.'

Holly nudges me. 'Maybe they've gone too far this time.'

I hold my breath.

Izzy laughs. 'You've seen my house. One bonus of having loaded parents is I get a huge allowance. And anyway, I wanted to get you something special. You've been through such a hard time lately.'

Eve starts to smile and my heart sinks. 'This is amazing,' she says. 'Seriously. I don't know how to thank you.'

'Oh, I'm sure I'll think of something,' Izzy says, with a sly grin in my direction.

I feel a weird shrinking sensation. Like someone's thrown a net around me and they're pulling it tight.

19

The next day, when Holly and I get to registration, Eve is sitting with Izzy, Vivien and Stephen, all of them hunched over her new iPad. They're watching a movie trailer and she's laughing her head off.

'I don't think I've ever seen Eve laugh before,' Holly says glumly as we take our seats.

'It looks so much fun,' Eve cries as the trailer comes to an end.

'Or sounding so happy,' I mutter. The Blood Witches have got Eve so relaxed in their company, surely it won't be long before they make their move and ask her to join them.

'We're going to see it at the cinema tonight,'

Izzy says to Eve. 'Why don't you come too?'

'Really?' Eve looks at Izzy with a mixture of shock and gratitude.

'Of course.'

I take my phone from my bag and do a quick search for the cinema listings. Unlike the multiplexes in London, there's only one screen in Fairhollow and only one movie showing.

'Oh my God, look at this!' I pass Holly the phone.

The movie showing tonight is called *Witch World*. *Imagine a world where witches rule*, the blurb reads. 'They must be going to ask her tonight,' I whisper. 'Seeing this movie together would give them the perfect excuse to bring up the subject of being Blood Witches.'

Holly passes the phone back to me. 'We're going to have to go too,' she says. 'We have to stop them.'

Usually, going to see a film is one of my favourite things to do – right up there with going to a gig or eating stuffed-crust pizza. But not tonight. As Holly and I make our way to the cinema, wearing baseball caps pulled down to our noses and coats buttoned up to our chins, it feels more like we're undercover cops on a stake-out and my whole body is tight with tension.

The Fairhollow Roxy is on the very outskirts of town, at the furthest end of the High Street and surrounded by fields and woods. Apparently it's been there since the 1920s and is one of the oldest cinemas in the country. As it looms up, ghostly white against the darkening sky, I can just imagine queues of men and women in 1920s-style clothes, waiting to see the latest black and white movie. Thankfully, as it's a Monday night, there are very few people around tonight, and no sign of the Blood Witches.

We hurry into the foyer. The floor is covered in a faded red carpet that's fraying in patches and a huge chandelier hangs from the centre of the ceiling. Half of its bulbs have gone. The whole place has a slightly haunted-house feel. I shiver and follow Holly over to the ticket booth.

'Where should we sit?' I ask as we walk into the darkened auditorium. We're the first ones in there so we have our pick.

'At the back,' Holly says, heading up the aisle. 'That way we can see all of the other seats and we'll be able to keep our eye on the Blood Witches.'

We head to some seats in the far corner and wait. The screen flickers into life and starts playing a series of cheesy adverts for local businesses.

'ABC Motors!' a man booms out at us. 'For all of your motoring needs. We won't *drive* you crazy.'

'Oh, please!' Holly groans. 'Who writes this stuff?'

The door creaks open and my heart leaps. A couple walk in and go and sit in the front row.

'Do you suffer from tension headaches?' a grinning woman wearing way too much make-up shrieks from the screen.

'Not until I heard your voice,' Holly mutters.

The door creaks open again. This time a group of people enter. As they walk past the light of the screen I see Izzy's silhouette – her perfect ringlets bobbing up and down. Eve is behind her with Vivien and Stephen following, holding tubs of popcorn.

Holly and I slide right down in our seats. Thankfully the adverts finish and the room is plunged into darkness. I watch as Izzy and the others head to the back of the cinema and start shuffling into a row in front of us. Thankfully, they stop in the middle of the row and sit down.

Then the movie begins. It's a comedy set in a small town in America where all of the girls are witches. But it's nothing like Fairhollow. These witches only ever seem to use their powers to do things like put on their make-up and tidy their bedrooms.

'This is so lame,' Holly whispers as the main character casts a spell to turn everything in her bedroom pink.

I nod, wondering what the Blood Witches must be making of it. I close my eyes and try to tune into the feelings coming from their direction. Anxiety starts fluttering in my ribcage like a trapped bird. I frown. Why would they be feeling nervous? Apart from the frightening amount of pink, this movie is hardly scary.

Finally the film comes to its predictable end at the school prom, where the main witch fills the dance floor with glitter and turns the grumpy head teacher into a toad.

'Oh, yawn!' Holly mutters. 'Turning people into toads is so last millennium.'

The Blood Witches, who've sat in silence throughout the whole thing, get to their feet. The fluttering in my ribcage builds to a crescendo.

'Do you want to come with us to our secret hideout?' I hear Izzy say.

'Oh, I don't know. It's getting a bit late,' Eve replies.

'Come on, don't be boring,' Vivien says.

'Yeah, we did buy your ticket and popcorn,' Stephen adds.

My heart starts pounding and this time I know

the nerves are my own. They must be going to ask Eve to join them tonight. That would explain why they're so nervous too. It hadn't dawned on me before, but I suddenly realise that there's a lot at stake for the Blood Witches right now too.

'OK. I'll come for a bit,' Eve says as they start heading down the aisle. She doesn't exactly sound super-keen.

Holly and I wait for them to get to the door then we leap up and follow them.

It's pitch dark outside apart from a thin crescent moon hanging in the sky. Izzy and the others are hurrying across the road, in the direction of the woods. Sticking to the shadows, we follow them to a narrow footpath, cutting in between the trees. We wait a couple of minutes then start heading up the path behind them, careful not to make a sound. The trees loom over us, like giants, waving their huge branch-arms in the breeze. I reach into my pocket for Mum's locket, hoping it will make me feel braver. But as soon as I wrap my fingers around it, an image flashes into my mind. It's of my mum, Celeste, stumbling up this same path. It's raining hard and the wind is lashing at her hair. I hear a cry. *Her* cry. And then it's gone. I stand still for a moment, trying to get my bearings.

'Are you OK?' Holly mouths to me.

I nod and carry on walking. What did I just see? Did my mum come here once? Why was she crying? I put the locket back in my pocket. I need to stay focused on Eve right now. I can't get distracted.

Up ahead of us, the pathway widens. Holly gestures at me to hide behind a huge oak tree. The Blood Witches have come to a standstill. My skin breaks into a cold sweat. What would they do if they saw us here? If they'd seen us in the cinema we could have just brushed it off as a coincidence but here? Here there's no excuse.

'Where are we?' Eve asks. She sounds fearful.

'Raven Lake,' Stephen replies.

'It's our special place,' Izzy says. 'No one else knows about it. Only you.'

'That's how much we trust you,' Vivien says.

'But do you trust us?' Izzy asks.

There's a moment of silence. I shift slightly and a twig cracks beneath my foot. My heart almost stops beating. Did they hear it? Will they see us?

'Of course I trust you,' Eve says.

If I wasn't too scared to make a sound, I'd breathe a sigh of relief.

'Good,' Izzy says. 'Because there's something we'd like to ask you.'

My heart is pounding so fast now I can hear the blood rushing in my ears. Holly looks at me, her eyes wide.

'What did you think of the movie?' Vivien says.

'The movie?' Eve sounds surprised. 'It was good. Fun.'

'Yes,' Izzy says, her voice now so sickly-sweet it's practically a purr. 'It is a lot of fun . . . being a witch.'

Eve laughs nervously.

'The most fun I've ever had,' Izzy continues.

'What – what do you mean?' Eve stammers.

I look at Holly and hold my breath.

'That's why we brought you here,' Izzy says. 'To let you know that the three of us . . . we're witches.'

'But I – I don't understand.'

Very slowly and very carefully, I peer out from behind the tree. Eve is standing staring at Izzy, barely visible in the pale moonlight.

'Oh, I think you do,' Izzy says softly. 'I saw what you did in the cave when we were trapped. I saw how you moved that rock. We know about your powers. But it's OK because we're exactly the same. We're witches too. And we want you to join us.'

'Your power is awesome,' Vivien says, taking a step towards Eve.

'It is seriously cool,' Izzy says. 'I wish I could do what you do.'

'Really?' Eve squeaks. 'But . . .' She turns away and I quickly shrink back behind the tree.

'I hate my power,' Eve says, more firmly this

time. 'I don't want to have it. I just want to have a normal life.'

'But normal's so boring,' Izzy says.

'Yeah, with our powers we can do anything,' Stephen says.

'Yes, we can. We can even heal your brother,' Izzy says.

Deep in the woods, a fox howls and then everything is silent.

20

I lean against the tree feeling dizzy. The words Izzy's saying feel all wrong. I can sense that she's lying.

'What?' Eve's voice rings out around the woods, causing something to flutter in the trees high above us. 'What do you mean, you can heal my brother?'

'Exactly that,' Izzy says. 'I have the power to heal people. If you join us, I'll make George get better.'

Holly starts shaking her head furiously.

I want to yell out 'liar' but I'm suddenly overcome with a terrible thought. Is this where Celeste came when she switched allegiances to the Blood Witches so that they would save my life? Is this where they told her they would heal me? Is that why I got the flashback of her here? I'm so dizzy with fear and confusion tiny pinpricks of light start flashing before my eyes.

'Oh, wow,' Eve gasps. 'I don't know what to say.'

'Say you'll join us,' Izzy murmurs.

'I – I . . . Can I think about it?'

'What's to think about?' Vivien says tersely. 'Do you want your brother to get better or not?'

'Yes of course I do,' Eve cries. 'It's just so much to take in.'

'I understand,' Izzy says. Her voice is still sickly-sweet but I can feel her anger and frustration burning its way across the ground towards me like a forest fire. 'Why don't we come back here at four o'clock tomorrow? If you want to join us, meet us here.'

'OK,' Eve says.

'You won't regret it,' Stephen says.

'No,' Izzy says. 'If you join us, you won't regret it at all.'

The dark implication behind her words hangs

heavy in the night air: *But if you don't join us, you'll regret it forever.*

'OK. Thank you. I'll – I'll see you then.' Eve starts heading back down the path towards us. Holly and I shrink back into the shadows behind the tree.

I hold my breath as she rushes past.

'Come on,' Izzy snaps to Vivien and Stephen. 'Let's go down to the lake.'

As soon as they've gone, Holly turns to me. 'Should we go after Eve?'

I shake my head. 'We need to tell Aunt Clara what's happened,' I whisper breathlessly. 'We need to ask her what to do.'

When we get back to Paper Soul there's a light on in the kitchen upstairs and the murmur of conversation. We burst into the room to see Mrs Schofield who runs the stationery shop next door sitting by Aunt Clara at the table. There's a pot of tea and a plate of biscuits in front of them.

'Hello, girls,' Aunt Clara says. 'Did you have a nice time at the cinema?'

'Yes, lovely,' I say, while sending Aunt Clara the psychic text message: *No, it was horrible and we need to talk!*

Aunt Clara stares at me for a moment. 'How lovely.' Her voice sounds slightly strained and I know she's got my message.

'So, do you think I ought to have the operation?' Mrs Schofield asks, helping herself to a refill from the teapot.

'Yes, I think you should.' Aunt Clara looks at Holly and me. 'Mrs Schofield's been having some problems with her varicose veins.'

'Oh, right,' I say calmly, while inside my head I'm screaming.

'This is lovely ginger tea, Clara,' Mrs Schofield says. 'So warming.'

Holly looks at me. I don't need to read her mind to know exactly what she's thinking.

'Didn't you say you needed me to help with your

homework, Nessa?' Aunt Clara says, giving me a pointed stare.

'What? Oh – yes! Yes, my History assignment.'

'History was my favourite subject when I was your age,' Mrs Schofield says, helping herself to a biscuit. 'I'd be happy to help too.'

'Oh no, that's fine,' Aunt Clara gets to her feet. 'I'm sure we've got it covered.' She looks at Mrs Schofield.

Mrs Schofield takes another sip of her tea.

Please go! I silently implore.

'Oh!' Mrs Schofield puts her cup down, looking slightly confused. 'I have to go.' She gets up and puts on her coat. 'Thank you very much for your advice, Clara. I'll see you tomorrow. Good night, girls.' She picks up her handbag and hurries out of the door.

Holly grins. 'OK, which one of you did that? Which one of you made her leave?'

Aunt Clara looks at me and smiles. 'I think it was both of us. Now, tell me, what happened?'

I sit down at the table and put my head in my hands. 'After the movie, they took Eve to their secret hideout and they asked her to join them.'

Aunt Clara looks horrified. 'And did she?'

I shake my head. 'Not yet.'

'She said she needed some time to think about it.' Holly starts pacing up and down the kitchen.

'But she's going to say yes,' I say glumly.

Aunt Clara sits down beside me. 'How do you know?'

'Because they've told her they can heal her brother.' I look at Aunt Clara, my eyes suddenly filling with tears. 'Is it true? Can they heal him? Are they doing what they did to my mum?' The tears spill on to my face.

'Oh, love.' Aunt Clara clasps my hands in hers. They feel warm and strong. 'No, no they can't. None of them are healers and the Blood Witch who healed you died a long time ago. They don't have a healer in this generation. Not yet anyway.'

'So, they were lying,' Holly hisses. 'Wow, they

really will stop at nothing to get what they want.'

'Yes, but this gives you an opportunity,' Aunt Clara says. 'If you can get to Eve and explain everything – if you can convince her that they're lying and they're not able to heal her brother – then she'll never join them.' Aunt Clara reaches out to take hold of Holly's hand too. 'You mustn't give up now, not when there's still hope.'

Holly nods. I feel a surge of strength coming from Aunt Clara's hand into my own and it slowly spreads throughout my body.

'Silver me, Silver you,' Aunt Clara begins and Holly and I join in, chanting the words as if our lives depended on it. 'Silver us, Silver true.'

21

Holly stays the night so that we can go and see Eve as soon as possible the next morning. It's the glummest, most stressful sleepover ever. Neither of us is able to sleep a wink but we're barely able to say a word either. We're too filled with dread at what might be about to happen so instead we toss and turn and stare up at the ceiling. We'd decided that eight o'clock was the earliest possible time we could call at Eve's house on a Saturday, so as soon as my alarm clock gets to seven thirty we leap out of bed and start pulling on our clothes.

Aunt Clara clearly didn't sleep well either. When we get to the kitchen she's fully dressed and sitting at the table with her collection of crystals laid out in a circle.

'For protection,' she says, when she sees me looking at them. 'I have a feeling we're going to be needing lots of that today.' She gets up and puts the kettle on. 'Can I get you girls some breakfast?'

I look at Holly and we both shake our heads.

'I just want to get it done,' I say. 'I just want to get to Eve's house.'

Aunt Clara nods. 'OK, but remember what happened last time. Don't rush in. Don't scare her off.'

'We won't,' Holly says. She looks pale from worry and lack of sleep. 'At least, I hope we won't.'

Aunt Clara hugs us both, then presses crystals into our hands. 'Take these. And good luck.'

As we race along the High Street my head's so full of thoughts about what to say to Eve that I don't even notice Niall setting up the tables and chairs on the pavement outside The Cup and Saucer.

'Hey,' he calls. 'Where's the fire?'

I stop in my tracks and stare at him. 'What fire?'

He laughs. 'I didn't mean literally. It's a saying – for when people are in a rush. Like they're running away from a fire.'

I feel a sudden burst of irritation. I'm tired of Niall thinking I'm just some stupid kid who's too young to play in a band and needs everything explaining. I can't be bothered to try any more – especially not when I've got something so much more important to think about.

'Sorry, I haven't got time to stop and chat,' I say coolly and hurry on.

'Is everything OK?' he calls out after me. He actually sounds concerned.

I pretend I don't hear him and carry on up the street. I feel a wave of confusion coming from Holly. I quickly block it out. I can't think of anything apart from Eve.

When we get to Eve's house all of the curtains are still drawn.

'What do you think we should do?' Holly asks as we pace up and down the pavement outside.

'I don't know.' I feel so jittery it's hard to think straight. 'They might like having lie-ins at the weekend. We don't want to annoy them by waking them up.'

'Let's wait for a bit,' Holly says, sitting down on the kerb.

As we wait, I run through possible conversation starters with Eve in my head. *Hey, I know we really upset you last time we came here but . . .* But what? *Now we're going to upset you even more and tell you that your brother can't be cured by the witches you think are your friends.*

I glance over at the house, the curtains in one of the downstairs rooms have been opened. I grab Holly's arm. 'I think they're up.'

We make our way along the path, my heart pounding.

'Who's going to speak?' Holly asks. 'You or me?'

'I will.' I press the doorbell and take a deep breath.

I hear the sound of footsteps inside the house and the door opens. Eve's mum stands in the doorway in her dressing down, holding a steaming mug.

'Yes?' she says, looking really confused. Then her expression darkens. 'Oh, it's you.'

'Yes, we – er – we were wondering if Eve was in,' I stammer.

'Why? So you can upset her again?'

I feel sharp bursts of anger flying through the air towards me. 'No! Not at all. We've got something really important to tell her.'

'It must be, to call at this time on a Saturday.'

'It is,' Holly says, stepping forwards. 'I swear to you that we're telling the truth, the whole truth and nothing but the truth.'

I stare at her. Why's she talking like she's in some kind of courtroom drama?

Eve's mum looks equally bemused. 'Is this some kind of prank? Because I can tell you right now that this is not a good time to be –'

'No!' I exclaim. 'It's not a prank at all. We need to speak to Eve.'

'Well, I'm afraid you're out of luck.' Eve's mum starts closing the door. 'She's not at home.' The door slams shut.

I look at Holly, frustrated. If Eve isn't here, then where is she?

22

As we hurry down the pathway Holly grabs my arm.

'Oh my God, do you think she's already made up her mind? Do you think she's not waiting until later and has gone to see Izzy?'

My throat tightens. If she has then we're too late. 'We need to find out. Come on, let's go to Izzy's house.'

Izzy's house is a huge gated mansion in the centre of a private estate. As I look at the darkened windows glinting down the driveway at me like soulless eyes I feel a rush of fear. Are the Blood Witches gathered in there now with Eve? Are they welcoming her to their circle?

'How are we going to find out if Eve's in there?' I say, looking through the bars of the gate in despair. The house is set so far back from the road it's impossible to see a thing.

Holly sighs. 'I guess we're just going to have to ask.'

'What?' I watch in horror as she presses the intercom button beside the gate. 'What are you doing?'

Before Holly can reply there's a click and the intercom crackles into life. 'Hello,' a man's voice says.

'Oh, hi there,' Holly says in a weird American accent. 'Could I speak with Izzy, please?'

'Izzy isn't here,' the man replies curtly.

'Oh gosh, darn it!' Holly exclaims. 'Do y'all know when she'll be back?'

'I have no idea. She's gone out for breakfast.'

'OK, thank you. Have a nice day!' Holly grabs my hands and starts hurrying up the street. 'Come on.'

'What was that accent about?' I say, running to keep up with her.

'To throw them off the scent,' Holly says. 'If Izzy's dad tells her an American stopped by, she won't have a clue it was us.'

'Right. Do you think she really has gone out to breakfast? Or do you think they've gone to the lake with Eve?'

'Only one way to find out,' Holly says.

I look at her blankly.

'This is Fairhollow,' Holly says. 'There's only one place people go for breakfast – The Cup and Saucer. Come on!'

When we get to The Cup and Saucer it's already quite busy.

'Let's pretend we're looking at the menu,' I say to Holly, 'And see if they're in there.'

We huddle around the menu in the window and peer into the café.

'There – at the back!' Holly exclaims.

Izzy, Stephen and Vivien are sat at a table at the

back of the café, hunched over in conversation. There's no sign of Eve.

'Yes!' says Holly. 'She's not with them.'

'But how do you know? She could be in the toilet – or at the counter.' I start searching the café and my eyes meet Niall's. He's heading towards the door, holding a tray of hot drinks. Damn!

'There's no fourth chair,' Holly says.

'What?'

Niall starts grinning at me.

'At their table,' Holly says. 'There's no fourth chair. Eve can't be with them. Unless they were making her stand, which would be very weird, even for the Blood Witches.'

I breathe a sigh of relief.

Niall comes out. 'Hello again. Can I get you guys a drink?'

'We have to go,' I say.

Niall looks confused. 'But you only just got here. You were looking at the menu.'

'Yeah, well, we changed our minds,' Holly says.

215

She links her arm with mine. 'Come on.'

Niall looks hurt. But I can't worry about that now. We still have a chance to stop the Blood Witches – if we can find Eve first.

'Let's try the library,' Holly says. 'That's where I go when I'm feeling confused.'

But when we get to the library it's full of parents and kids and there's no sign of Eve.

We look in the park and the sweet shops and we even go up to the school, just in case Eve felt the random urge to go there on a Saturday but there's still no sign of her.

'We need to get inside her mind,' Holly says as we trudge past the station. 'How will she be feeling right now?'

'Confused? Scared? Stressed?' I offer.

Holly nods. 'Right. So where would you want to go if you were confused, scared or stressed?'

I think of all the times I've felt confused and scared since I got to Fairhollow. 'If I couldn't go to the oak tree, I'd go back home, with my dad,' I say.

'But that's not possible because he's on the other side of the world and our house is being rented out to strangers so –'

'That's it!' Holly's eyes gleam with excitement.

'It is?' I look at her blankly.

'Eve's family came to Fairhollow after George's accident but they lived in Newbridge before, right?'

'Right.'

'So maybe she's gone back there to try to get her head straight.'

I feel a glimmer of excitement. It would make sense. And Newbridge's only one train stop away so it would be easy for her to do. Holly and I both look over at the station.

'The next train to arrive on platform one will be the 11.06 to Newbridge,' the announcer's voice crackles.

'Oh my God, it's a sign,' Holly says. 'Come on!'

We race into the station, grab tickets and jump on to the train.

23

Ten minutes later, we're in Newbridge. It's only when we're standing on its bustling High Street, where a market is in full swing, that it dawns on me that this could be a lot harder that we'd thought. For a start, we don't have a clue where Eve used to live.

But luckily Holly looks like she knows exactly what to do. 'Follow me,' she says.

'Do you know her old address?' I ask, following her past a fish stall.

'Fresh mackerel straight off the boat!' the stallholder calls after us.

'No, but I think I know who will,' Holly replies.

'Who?'

'The post office.'

Holly leads me past cake stalls and clothes stalls and a huge stall selling crates of fruit and veg, and finally we reach the post office. Inside is so peaceful compared to the hustle and bustle of the market. There's just the gentle hum of chatter coming from two women behind the counter.

'Good morning,' Holly says in a ridiculously posh voice. She goes over to one of the post office staff, an elderly lady with cheeks as red and shiny as apples. 'I was wondering if you could help us. My sister and I have been away for many years on digs with our archaeologist father. Egypt, Peru, Botswana – you name it, we've dug it. Anyway, we're just back in Newbridge for the day and we wanted to look up a long-lost friend of ours – Eve Hart. But we can't quite remember where she lives.'

The woman frowns and I feel a stab of despair. Why does Holly have to go so over the top all the time?

'Eve Hart?' the woman says.

'Yes. She has an older brother, George. Lovely fellow.'

'Oh! I know who you mean. The Harts up on Cherry Hill.' The woman's face falls. 'So you won't have heard, then.'

'Heard what, my good lady?' Holly says.

I have to cross my arms to stop myself nudging her.

'He was in a terrible accident. Lost the use of his legs.'

Holly clasps her hands together. 'Oh no! We must go there immediately and offer our condolences. Cherry Hill, you say?'

'Yes, but you won't find them there I'm afraid. They moved away last year, after the accident. Needed to get away from it all, I suppose.'

Holly starts making her way to the door. 'OK. Thank you.'

The woman behind the counter gets to her feet. 'I could see if we have a forwarding address for them on file.'

'Oh no, it's OK, thank you,' Holly says, opening the door.

I race out after her, my face burning. 'Right, that is it!'

'What?'

'From now on, I do the talking.'

'But –'

'But nothing! We are not Victorians!'

I see a woman walking towards us, pushing a pram. 'Excuse me. Could you tell us the way to Cherry Hill?'

The woman gives us directions and carries on up the street. I turn back to Holly. 'There, see? No need for any weird accent, or stories about digging in Peru.'

Holly huffs. 'Yeah, but it was so much more boring.'

Cherry Hill is a five-minute walk from the High Street. It's full of quaint little cottages with beautifully designed front gardens. All of them are immaculately kept, apart from the one at the far end, with a For Sale sign, which is overgrown with long grass and wild flowers.

'Do you think that's it?' I whisper to Holly as we get closer.

Holly nods. 'It looks like a good place to start.'

We make our way up the rambling front garden and peer through the grimy glass panel in the front door. The inside of the cottage is steeped in darkness.

'Let's check round the back,' I whisper to Holly.

We creep round to the side of the house and let ourselves through a gate. The back garden is even more overgrown than the front. The grass is almost knee-high and in the flower beds daffodils and bluebells are fighting their way through a tangled mess of weeds. Then I see a sight that makes my heart skip a beat. There, at the bottom of the garden, sitting beneath a huge oak tree, is Eve. I nudge Holly.

'Let's take it really slowly this time,' I whisper. 'We mustn't scare her off.'

Holly nods and we start making our way through the long grass towards her.

When we get a few metres away I cough. Eve jumps and turns round.

'What . . .? How . . .? What are you doing here?' she gasps.

'We need to talk to you,' I say softly.

'We know what happened,' Holly says.

'What do you mean?' Eve stares up at us fearfully.

I crouch down in front of her and Holly does the same.

'We know Izzy has asked you to join them,' I say.

'Oh.' Eve looks down.

'We just want you to know what you'd be getting into,' I say.

'We want you to know how evil they are,' Holly adds.

'Evil?' Eve laughs. 'They're not evil. They're my friends.'

Holly gives a sarcastic cough. I frown at her. We mustn't make Eve go on the defensive.

'I know they've raised a lot of money to help your brother,' I say.

'Yes – they have,' Eve cuts in. 'And that's not all they're going to do for him.'

'They can't be trusted,' I say. 'They only want to use their powers to hurt people and to do bad things.'

'That's not true!' Eve scrambles to her feet, her eyes glinting with anger. 'They're going to help George. They're going to make him get better. And I'm going to join them.' She stares at us defiantly.

'But they're only using you,' Holly says. 'If you join them, they'll only be one away from completing their pente and when they do that, they'll get all the power and they'll make everyone's lives hell. Listen, there are two kinds of witches – Blood Witches and Silver Witches. Silver Witches only use their powers for good. Blood Witches are evil. And each new generation has a chance to gain power over the other. The first group to complete a 'pente' of five witches will win. You need to join us, the

Silver Witches, so that we can beat them.'

'You're lying!' Eve is looking so angry it makes my heart plummet. The Blood Witches have won. All of their scheming has paid off. I think of them sitting in the classroom. Vivien laughing as she told Izzy how she mimicked the doctor and I feel sick.

'We're not lying,' I say, standing up. 'You have to believe us.'

'Yes, you are!' Eve pushes me out of her way. But instead of running up the garden away from us she stays rooted to the spot, her face turning chalk-white. For a split second, my mind goes completely blank.

'What . . .? But . . .' Eve gasps – before collapsing to the ground.

'What just happened?' Holly says, pulling her phone from her pocket.

Slowly, the fog in my brain starts to lift. What *did* just happen?

'I'll call an ambulance,' Holly says, turning her phone on.

But before she can start to dial, Eve starts moving and moaning.

'Are you OK?' I drop down to my knees and gently place my hand on her shoulder.

'I saw them,' Eve gasps. 'When I touched you. I saw them.'

'You saw who?' I say.

'Vivien and the others. She was laughing. She

was saying . . .' Eve breaks off looking close to tears. 'She was saying she pretended to be the doctor. *She* told my mum there was no hope for George.'

'That's what happened!' Holly crouches down and looks at Eve. 'But how did you see that?' She turns to me. 'Did you make her see your memory?'

'I think so.' I glance at Eve. 'I'm an empath. That's my power. It sometimes lets me see flashbacks from other people's lives and I think I just made you see a flashback from mine.'

'Try showing her some more,' Holly urges.

I look at Eve. 'Would that be OK?'

Eve nods. I close my eyes and grip her shoulder tightly. I picture a montage of memories of all the times Izzy and the others have shown their true colours to me. I feel Eve cringing beside me but I carry on. And then I'm overcome by a feeling of nausea so strong I have to let go of Eve's shoulder and lie down. I stare up at the clear blue sky, breathing deeply until I feel OK again.

Next to me, I hear Eve scrambling to her feet.

'Are you guys OK?' Holly asks anxiously.

I stand up and look at Eve. Her face is flushed and she looks furious.

'How could they do that? How could they lie to me like that?' She stares at a nearby apple tree and there's a terrible cracking sound.

'Watch out!' Holly cries, pushing us both to one side. The tree topples down. Landing right where I'd been lying.

'Oh no!' Eve cries. 'Oh no!' She starts to sob. 'I'm so sorry. I didn't mean to . . . I hate this power. I hate it!'

Holly and I both place a hand on her shoulders.

'If it's any consolation, we both hated our powers at first too,' I say.

'Really?' Eve looks at me through tear-filled eyes.

'Yeah, but you soon get used to it,' Holly says.

Eve shakes her head and starts crying even harder. 'But you don't understand. I don't want to get used to it. How can I after what I did to George?'

'What do you mean?' I ask gently.

'I'm the reason George is in a wheelchair,' Eve says, wiping the tears from her face. 'My stupid power put him there.'

'How?'

'We were having an argument in the car. He said I couldn't use his PlayStation and it made me really mad. I was looking at this post by the roadside and suddenly it came crashing down. I could have killed him. And I could have killed you just now, with the tree.'

'But it wasn't your fault,' I say.

'I caused mayhem before I learnt to control my power,' Holly says.

'Did you put anyone you love in a wheelchair?'

'No, but . . .' Holly breaks off and looks at me helplessly.

'I'm going to have to join them,' Eve says, looking distraught. 'They've promised me they'll cure him. I won't be able to live with myself if I turn down even the chance to make him better.'

I feel overcome with sorrow, realising that this

must have been exactly how my mum would have felt about me. 'But they're lying. None of them are healers. None of them have that power. They're just saying whatever it takes to get you to join them.'

'But what if they get a healer?' Eve says. 'What if they find another witch with that power?'

'Well, I guess that's a decision you have to make.' I feel empty. Empty of words and empty of hope. 'Maybe we should leave you for a bit, to think about it.' If we keep on begging Eve it might end up pushing her away. If we give her some time on her own, she might come round. I gesture at Holly to follow me down the garden. My heart feels heavier with every step.

But just as we reach the gate Eve calls out to us. 'Wait! I've made my decision.'

25

Slowly, my heart thumping, I turn to face Eve.

'I know I can't ignore my power any more,' she says, clenching her hands into fists. 'I know I have to accept that I'm a witch.'

I can hardly breathe as I wait for what's coming next.

'I feel so guilty over what I did to George,' Eve says.

My heart sinks. That's it, then. It's all over.

'But I'd feel even guiltier if I joined them.'

'What?' I stare at Eve, hardly daring to believe what this means.

Eve unclenches her fists and gives me a weak smile. 'I want to join you. I want to learn how to use my powers for good. If I join them, they'll make me use them for evil and I wouldn't be able to live with myself.'

'Yes!' Holly leaps at Eve and flings her arms around her. 'This is going to be so great, isn't it, Nessa?'

I nod, too overcome with relief to speak. Eve is going to join us. She's going to join us, not the Blood Witches. I walk over to Eve, filling with gratitude. 'Thank you,' I say quietly. 'Thank you so much.'

Eve looks at her watch. 'Right, I'm going to tell them.'

Holly frowns. 'Are you sure? You could just not turn up.'

Eve shakes her head. 'No. I want to tell them exactly what I think of them.'

Holly grins. 'Cool.'

We get the next train back to Fairhollow. On the way I feel happier and happier as the full meaning of what's happened sinks in. I send a quick text to Aunt Clara.

232

Great news! Eve's joining us! Xoxo

She texts back straight away. **Fantastic!!!!!!!!**
She must have been waiting by her phone for news
all day.

When we get back to Fairhollow it's almost
four o'clock. We race down to the end of the
High Street, past the cinema, where the matinee
crowd is spilling out on to the street, and up the
track into the woods. Instantly it grows darker, as
the branches intertwine into a roof high above us,
keeping out the light. For the first time since Eve's
said she'll join us I feel afraid. The Blood Witches
are hardly going to be happy at the news. What
if they try to force Eve to join them? I wrap my
fingers around Mum's locket and feel a surge of
strength. The Blood Witches might have forced
Mum to join them but they're not going to do it
to Eve. I'm not going to let them. When the path
starts to widen, Eve goes on ahead of us. I can see
three figures silhouetted against the lake. They've

233

lit a fire. Shadows are dancing around them like black ghosts.

'You came!' Vivien exclaims as Eve approaches them.

'I knew she would,' Izzy says calmly.

'In darkness we live,' Stephen starts chanting, 'in darkness we fall.'

Izzy and Vivien join in as they stand in a line, facing Eve. 'Darkness for Blood, darkness to all!'

'I don't think so,' Eve says.

I look at Holly and she nods. We start walking towards them.

'Oh no, what are those freaks doing here?' Stephen says as soon as he sees us.

'We're with Eve,' I reply. We're just a couple of metres from them now. Close enough to see Izzy's eyes glinting with rage.

'What do you mean, you're with Eve?' She turns her glare on Eve. 'Did you bring them here? Did you show them our secret hideout?'

'Oh, calm down,' Holly says. 'We already knew

all about your "secret" hideout. We followed you here after the cinema last night.'

Rage is pouring from Izzy now like red-hot lava. I picture myself surrounded by a wall of ice to block it.

'I know what you did,' Eve says, her voice cracking with emotion. 'I know how you lied to me and my mum.' She turns and looks at Vivien. 'Nessa showed me what you said about mimicking the doctor.'

Vivien's mouth opens and closes like a goldfish's. 'She showed you? How?'

'It's one of the things empaths can do,' I say breezily.

'One of the *many* things empaths can do,' Holly adds. 'So much cooler than being a boring old mimic.'

Vivien's face flushes. She looks at Izzy as if to say, *What do we do now?*

Izzy takes a step towards Eve. 'But what about poor George?' she says slyly. 'If you don't join us he'll never get better. We're the only ones who can cure him.'

'Liar!' Eve spits.

Izzy takes a step back in shock.

'None of you are healers,' Eve says. 'But you're all liars and I don't want anything more to do with you.'

'Now, wait a minute.' Izzy narrows her eyes and stares at Eve. 'It's not that easy. You can't just walk away from us. We're the Blood Witches.'

'Oh, really?' Eve glances at a tall thin tree over to our right. Holly and I instinctively step back. A loud crack rings out around the woods as the tree crashes to the ground, falling right between us and the Blood Witches. I look through the branches at them. They're rooted to the spot in shock. Holly stares at the fire by their feet and the flames start leaping higher and higher. The Blood Witches stumble back, towards the lake.

YOU WILL NEVER WIN! I picture the words flying from my mind, over the fallen tree,

236

through the flames and into their heads.

'No!' Izzy yells.

YES! I project back at her.

'Get away from here!' Izzy cries.

'With pleasure,' Holly replies, looking at the fire. The flames give one last leap and then flicker back down to their previous size.

I grab hold of Eve and Holly's hands and we start striding back through the woods. 'Welcome to the Silver Witches,' I say, giving Eve's hand a squeeze.

'Thank you!' She smiles at me and squeezes my hand back.

'Let's teach her the incantation,' Holly says.

I nod and we start to chant. 'Silver me, Silver you, Silver us, Silver true.' Louder and louder, until it feels as if the whole woods is ringing with our voices.

'This calls for a celebration,' Holly says as we make our way back along the High Street. 'Milkshakes?'

Of course, the first person I see when we get to The Cup and Saucer is Niall. He's wiping down one of the tables outside. He looks really worried. 'All right?' he says cautiously.

Holly sighs but as she and Eve disappear into the café I stop and grin. The Silvers now have three, the same as the Blood Witches, and things are *so* much better than just all right. 'Yes, great, thanks.'

Niall looks really relieved. 'So, I was thinking . . .' he says.

'Yes?' We're even with the Blood Witches. Now we're just as likely to complete our pente first.

'Would you like to go and see a movie?'

'What?' I stare at him in shock.

'With me?' Niall smiles shyly. 'Would you like to go and see a movie? With me. There's one on at the moment that's supposed to be pretty good. Something about witches . . .'

I burst out laughing. And once I start laughing I can't stop. All the tension of the past few weeks comes spilling out with every giggle.

'OK, so that wasn't exactly the reaction I'd been hoping for.' Niall's cheeks flush red and he turns away.

'Oh no, I wasn't laughing at you.' I take a deep breath and try to compose myself. 'I would love to go to a movie with you,' I say with a grin. 'Especially one about witches.'

What's YOUR witching power?
Take the quiz!

Question 1.
What's your favourite subject at school?

A) History. You love dreaming about how romantic the past was.

B) PE. You're on every team going!

C) Lunch. You love catching up with your friends.

D) French. You'd love to be able to speak other languages and travel the world.

E) English. You're always stuck in a book!

Question 2.
How long does it take you to get ready in the morning?

A) 30 minutes – and that's just your hair!

B) Less than five minutes. You just throw your hair in a ponytail and go.

C) An hour. It takes time to put together the perfect outfit!

D) It depends – you're always trying new looks.

E) 15 minutes. You like to look natural, but not a mess!

Question 3.
How do you like to spend your weekends?

A) Having a DIY spa day with your best friends.

B) Playing rounders in the park or swimming at the beach.

C) Hitting the shops with your mates.

D) Going to a gig to watch a new band.

E) Curled up with a good book.

Question 4.
How would you ask your crush on a date?

A) Slip him a note in class.

B) Ask him after you score the winning goal in your football match.

C) Just go over and ask him!

D) Arrange a fun treasure hunt, and ask him at the end.

E) Text him, and play it cool.

Question 5.
What's your favourite thing to do at a sleepover?

A) Make DIY face masks and paint each other's nails.

B) Stay up all night playing video games.

C) Stalk your crush on Facebook.

D) Play an epic game of Truth or Dare.

E) Snuggle up and watch your favourite films.

Question 6.
What pictures are on your Instagram?

A) Cute #OOTD pictures.

B) Videos of you doing somersaults on the trampoline!

C) Silly selfies with all your friends.

D) Beautiful landscapes.

E) Inspirational quotes that mean something to you.

Question 7.
How would you describe your style?

A) Girly.

B) Sporty.

C) Casual and fun.

D) It's always changing!

E) Classic and vintage.

Question 8.
Who would you think is Cute-With-A-Captial-C?

A) You fall for a new guy each week!

B) The captain of the rugby team.

C) Someone who is charming and popular.

D) The mysterious guy at the back of the class.

E) Someone who seems tough on the outside, but is sweet underneath.

How did you score?

Mostly As

You're a TIME TURNER! You're a bit of a romantic, and you need more time in your day to plan the perfect way to catch that cute boy's eye. Slowing down time will help you make that romantic gesture, and win his heart!

Mostly Bs

You're an ENERGY HARNESSER! You're full of beans, and you're never happy sitting still. Your power will make everything around you as energetic as you are – just be careful not to set things on fire!

Mostly Cs

You're a MIMIC! You're at your happiest when you're surrounded by friends and having a good gossip. Being a mimic is perfect for playing pranks on your friends and sharing secrets!

Mostly Ds

You're TELEKINETIC! You're very independent and like to do things your own way. Being telekinetic means that you can get rid of any barriers in your path, and dance to the beat of your own drum!

Mostly Es

You're an EMPATH! You're calm, a good listener, and always there for your friends. Your power will help you understand exactly how people are feeling, and you'll even be able to speak in their heads!

Even more Monsters, Mysteries, Magic and Legends

Available in all good bookshops and online